John Harrold.

This book belongs to

. . . .

CONTENTS

Cover illustrated by Stuart Trotter.
Endpapers illustrated by John Harrold.

THE RUPERT ANNUAL

EXPRESS NEWSPAPERS

First published in Great Britain 2023 by Farshore
An imprint of HarperCollins*Publishers*
1 London Bridge Street, London SE1 9GF
www.farshore.co.uk

HarperCollins*Publishers*
Macken House, 39/40 Mayor Street Upper, Dublin 1, D01 C9W8, Ireland

ISBN 978 0 00 853710 4
Printed in UAE
001

Adult supervision is always necessary when a child is cooking or using sharp implements.

MIX
Paper | Supporting
responsible forestry
FSC™ C007454

FSC
www.fsc.org

RUPERT
CLASSIC

No. 88

RUPERT'S PICTURE PUZZLE

This picture was painted by Alex Cubie for Rupert's Adventure Series. It shows Rupert and his Mummy playing in a game which you can join in too. Every letter in the alphabet is represented by at least one of the objects in this room. Can you write down what they all are?

RUPERT
and the
PIPER

Telling how
the finding of
an old musical
pipe leads
Rupert through
one more
adventure.

RUPERT FINDS A PIPE

Here's Rupert with a pipe to blow;
It was his Uncle's long ago.

He starts to practise in a tree;
How strange! His Uncle he can see.

Once home his suitcase lid he lifts;
A book and rock are Rupert's gifts.

The book tells of the Piper Pied
Who drew all children to his side.

There is nothing that Rupert likes better than to help his mother explore the lumber room. One day he comes across a curious old musical pipe. "Good gracious," cries Mrs Bear, "I haven't seen that for ages. It's your Uncle Bruno's." Rupert goes up the road to find a quiet place for his music, and decides to climb into a tree for privacy. He hears distant footsteps and a well-known figure appears down the road.

When they have arrived at Mrs Bear's cottage, Uncle Bruno opens his case, and to Rupert's excitement he begins to bring out presents. "It's strange that you should have been playing that pipe," says Uncle Bruno, "for I've brought you a book all about a Piper who played one – The Pied Piper of Hamelin." Sitting on the arm of a chair, he listens while Uncle Bruno tells all about the Pied Piper and his wonderful pipe.

RUPERT FOLLOWS ALGY

Now Rupert in the rock bites deep,
Then strangely tired, he seems to sleep.

Some music quaint disturbs his ease;
His friends all running fast he sees.

So Rupert says, "I must give chase,"
And there begins a furious race.

A lake he is surprised to find,
But daren't stop lest he's left behind.

Soon Uncle Bruno has to go, and Rupert wonders what to do. Strangely enough, he doesn't feel very brisk. Usually he runs out to find his pals, but now his feet seem heavy, so he decides to curl up in the arm chair and look at the pictures of the Pied Piper. Hardly knowing how he got there, he finds himself leaning out of the window. To his astonishment, he sees his pals, Bill, Edward, Algy and the rest tearing away across the common in single file.

Burning with curiosity, Rupert pauses only to snatch up his scarf before rushing out of the house in pursuit of his pals. On goes the chase until Rupert feels he must drop with fatigue. Suddenly the track leads over the top of a crag, and a wonderful view opens out of trees and a wide lake with great mountains beyond. "Good gracious, why didn't I know of this place before?" pants the little bear. "Bill and Edward seem to know the way."

RUPERT JUMPS ON BOARD

He hears a Piper's music play,
And sees his friends all led away.

He calls the Piper, and protests;
"Oh," laughs the man, "they're all my guests!"

The Piper blows his pipe again,
And Rupert can't resist its strain.

He knows they've made a bad mistake
When they are rowed across the lake.

Rupert catches up with the whole party as they are entering a boat. "Hi!" he cries to the strange figure in black and white, "who are you and what are you doing to my pals?" "Why, I'm the Pied Piper, of course," grins the other, "and I've decided to take your pals away to my castle." "But you mustn't do that," gasps Rupert. "Their mothers will get terribly worried." "No one can resist my pipe," says the man. "I can do just as I like."

Rupert desperately tries to persuade his friends to return with him, but they all follow the Piper into the boat as if they were in a dream. "There's only one thing for it," thinks the little bear. "I must return to Nutwood for help." As he turns to run, a note from the pipe rings out clear and sweet behind him. It is the first time he has heard it so close at hand. At once he seems to lose all power and is drawn back towards the boat.

He sees a post beside a weir,
And, gathering all his strength, jumps clear.

A bird, approaching, hears him call,
Get me that branch before I fall."

And so, he wriggles up the bough,
Oh, can he save his friends, and how?

A squirrel squeaks, "Now drop that plan,
And hurry home fast as you can."

The boat goes faster and faster, and to his horror he sees that they are approaching a weir. Gathering all his strength, he leaps on to one of the posts at the top of the weir. There is a flapping of wings as a big bird flies up in curiosity. "Oh, please," cries the little bear, "do you think you can bring that branch down to me? I shall get drowned if I try to get off this post in any other way." With a squawk the bird makes off.

To Rupert's relief the bird soon returns with two others, and together they alight on the branch, weighing it down until it is within reach of the little bear. Half-way down the tree he meets a squirrel. "Oh, do tell me," cries the little bear, "do you know where the Piper has gone and how I can get to him?" The squirrel stares at him in astonishment. "You don't know what you're asking," he gasps. "If you'll take my advice you'll turn round."

RUPERT MEETS NEW FRIENDS

But since insistently he pleads,
The squirrel to a tunnel leads.

The Piper's castle lies that way,
And lights are shining bright as day.

The tunnel ends, the boat is there –
But empty; Rupert's in despair.

A lizard says, "Now don't have shocks!
Your friends are near; jump in that box."

In spite of the squirrel's words Rupert insists that he wants to go after his pals and to try to rescue them, so after a short while the little creature consents to show him the way. "There," says the squirrel, "that is the way to the Piper's castle, but I warn you the tunnel is difficult and dangerous." To his surprise he gets on without much difficulty, for electric bulbs set in the rock give a little light.

Before him, floating on the dark water, is the boat, but it is empty! Suddenly out of a far corner comes a tiny chuckle of laughter. Following the sound Rupert discovers a large lizard smiling at him. "So you're searching for your pals," says the queer creature. "Come with me. I'll show you the way." And he leads Rupert to where a sort of box is let into the rock, and tells him to get in.

RUPERT MEETS THE GIANT

There comes a jerk, a movement swift,
And Rupert's pulled up in a lift.

The liftman, who's a giant wise,
Hears Rupert's story with surprise.

And carries him, in one great hand,
Close to the Piper's castle grand.

Across a bridge and through a door,
His friends walk, dreaming as before.

The lift does not lead into a castle. It stops with a jolt and he finds himself again in the open air and facing an enormous giant who is grasping a heavy iron chain, and who looks surprised at seeing the little bear. "Whenever I hear anybody in the lift I pull it up," says the giant, "but who are you and what do you want?" Despite his size he looks quite a kindly giant, so Rupert plucks up courage and tells him all his story.

The giant can hardly believe the adventures that Rupert has been through to find his pals. He takes the little bear up in his great hand and walks a short way until the turrets and battlements of a huge castle come in sight. Thanking the giant for his information, he hurries away towards the castle. To his joy, Bill and Edward are still in sight, trudging steadily onward. Rupert cries out to them to stop but they still seem to be in a sort of dream.

RUPERT GETS THE MESSAGE

He follows, but, to his dismay,
The drawbridge moves and folds away.

He turns back, then, with heavy tread,
When something whizzes past his head.

A note from Bill says, "Help us out."
"They've seen him; Rupert gives a shout:

"Back to the giant I must run,
To ask him just what can be done."

Rupert is terribly disappointed that his pals don't seem to hear him, and there is nothing for him to do but to follow. As he reaches the level the drawbridge is pulled away from him, leaving him stranded on a little platform and cut off from the castle. While he is wondering how he can possibly get home his thoughts are interrupted by a swishing sound, and something whizzes by his head. "Whatever is that, and where's it come from?" he mutters.

Hastily unrolling the paper, he sees to his excitement that on it is the handwriting of his friend Bill Badger. The letter from Bill has roused Rupert from his despair. He thinks hard and then an idea comes to him. "That huge giant," he murmurs, "he seemed a friendly person, although he was one of the Piper's servants. Perhaps he would suggest something." It seems the only hope, and he races back until the great figure comes in sight again.

RUPERT TAKES A JOURNEY

The giant laughs, "Could you get in
The castle secretly, you'd win."

And then he makes, with special care,
A parachute for Rupert Bear.

With this contraption he can drop
If thrown above the castle top.

So, while to this strong aid he clings,
The giant sways him back, then flings.

The writing on the paper is too small for the giant to read, but Rupert eagerly tells him all about it and begs for help. The giant, however, only laughs loudly. "But is there any way in?" asks the little bear. Without answering, the giant busies himself with a clean handkerchief and some string, and then holds up the result and smiles mysteriously. "You've made a sort of parachute," says Rupert, puzzled. "How will that help me?"

"You forget that I am a giant and have a giant's strength. I could *throw* you over the castle; then, when you are above the highest tower you could let out the parachute and join your friends without the Piper knowing. Now then, tell me – dare you try it?" "All right, I'll do it," he says. At once the great arm is flung across, and the little bear finds himself whizzing through the cold air, straight and true in the direction of the castle.

RUPERT SHARES HIS ROCK

Upon the tower his comrades gasp;
The parachute's torn from his grasp!

He panics, then the rush of air
Stops, and he wakens in his chair!

His mother says, "You've dreamed, because
You ate that rock without a pause."

To share his rock he now thinks best,
And all his friends join in with zest.

The wind fills the giant's handkerchief with such force that it is dragged out of his hands, and he hurtles over the top of the tower without it. For a few seconds Rupert is in complete panic. Then gradually things seem to change. He flings out his arms and clutches something soft. Opening his eyes, he finds that he is struggling in his own armchair and in his own cottage. His book falls with a clatter. For a while he lies still and stares about in amazement.

"You've been having a bad dream," says Mrs Bear. "You must have eaten too much Sandybay Rock before reading about the Pied Piper." Without waiting, he goes to collect his friends and shares out the rest of the Sandybay Rock among them. Then he tells them all about the boat and the Piper and the squirrel and the cave and the giant and the castle. "Oooh. what a topping adventure," cries Bill Badger. "Well, I'm jolly glad it's all over," laughs Rupert.

Odd One Out

Look carefully at these drawings of Ottoline, Bill Badger and Edward.
Sort them out into matching pairs and put a circle round the odd ones out.

RUPERT and

*Rupert and Bill decide that they
Will go out walking for the day . . .*

It is a sunny morning, at the start of the holidays and Rupert and Bill have decided to go on a long hike . . . "Let's try somewhere different!" says Bill. "How about heading for the Lake?" "Good idea!" agrees Rupert. "If we take the path through the woods it will be even more of an adventure." The pair continue until they reach the edge of the trees. "Straight ahead!" says Bill. "All we have to do is keep on going in the same direction . . ."

the Water Bottle

"This way!" says Rupert. Bill agrees,
"The map showed a path through the trees."

"Look, Rupert! There's a hollow tree!"
"A hideaway! Let's go and see . . ."

As Rupert and Bill follow the path through the
woods, they spot a hollow, old tree. "Look at that!"
calls Bill. "It's like Robin Hood's hideaway! I'm
sure I could climb inside." To his delight, Rupert's
chum finds that the tree is even bigger than it
looked. "We'll both be able to fit in here!" he cries.
"Come on, Rupert! Let's see if it's dry. It will be
just the place for a secret camp. I'll mark it on the
map, so we can be sure of finding it again."

"There's lots of room. I'm sure that you
Will fit inside the tree trunk too . . ."

RUPERT'S PAL MAKES A DISCOVERY

"These leaves feel like a bed! I mean,
They're springy, like a trampoline!"

Then, suddenly, to Bill's dismay,
He feels the leafy floor give way . . .

Bill tumbles through an old trap door
And lands with a bump on the floor . . .

He clambers up and looks around –
Astonished at what he has found.

Inside the tree, Bill finds a mass of dry leaves, which have been blown in by the wind. "It's like a huge nest!" he calls. "I wonder how long all these have been piling up? They feel soft and springy, like a mattress . . ." Jumping up and down on the leaves, Bill suddenly feels the floor start to give way. "Help!" he cries. Rupert leans forward to grab his chum's arm, but it is too late. With a despairing wail, Bill sinks down through the leaves and disappears from sight . . .

To Bill's amazement, he falls down through the leaves into an underground chamber. Clambering to his feet, he peers around in the gloom. "It's a secret room!" he gasps. "There must have been a hidden trap-door . . ." The chamber is full of odd-looking bottles and jars. There are candles too and a heavy metal cauldron. Everything Bill sees is dusty and covered in cobwebs. "Rupert!" he calls. "Wait till you see what we've found. I think it's some sort of hide-out!"

RUPERT EXPLORES THE HIDE-OUT

"Rupert!" cries Bill. "Come down and see –
We've made a great discovery!"

"It's someone's hide-out! What a find!
Let's look at what they've left behind . . ."

"Whose are these books and ancient charts?"
"A wizard, versed in magic arts . . ."

"This bottle's full! It might just be
A magic potion! Shall we see?"

"Are you all right?" asks Rupert as his chum reappears. "Never felt better!" smiles Bill. "Come and have a look! There are stones, set in the wall, you can climb down, like steps . . ." "What a find!" blinks Rupert. "If the trap-door hadn't given way, we'd never have known it was here." "That's right!" nods Bill. "Whoever built this certainly meant to keep it well-hidden. Funny place to make a home, isn't it? Judging by all the cobwebs, I don't think it's been used for years . . ."

As the two chums start exploring the secret chamber they can hardly believe the things they find. "There are books and charts," says Rupert. "Flasks and bottles too!" says Bill. "I think it's some old wizard's lair!" "You might be right!" agrees Rupert. "We'd better not touch anything, in case he comes back." "There's no harm in just looking," says Bill. Picking up a glass bottle, he suddenly notices that it is still full. "Magic potion!" he cries excitedly. "I wonder what it does?"

"Be careful Bill! You might just find
The stuff's a poison of some kind . . ."

"Don't worry! I'll just pour a drop
To make a spell and then we'll stop . . ."

"That's odd, Rupert! You saw me pour
The bottle out, but now there's more . . ."

"It's like a magic trick – somehow
The water's back inside it now . . ."

Bill is so excited by his find that he carries the bottle out of the secret room and removes its silver stopper . . . "Be careful!" warns Rupert. "It could be poisonous, for all you know." "Don't worry," says Bill. "I'll only tip some on the grass. Wouldn't it be fun if it really was a magic potion? I know, let's try making a spell as well. Oh, potion show what you can do, please turn the grass from green to blue . . ." "Not that much!" gasps Rupert. "You've nearly emptied the bottle!"

Bill stops pouring and looks at the liquid in the bottle. "I've hardly used a drop!" he says. "In fact, I'm sure the level hasn't fallen at all . . ." "You're right!" blinks Rupert. "But that's impossible! I saw you tip out the whole lot. Look at the wet patch on the ground. It took more than a drop to do that!" "How odd!" says Bill. "It must be a trick bottle. Not as good as a magic potion but still quite a find! Perhaps we ought to take it back to show to Tigerlily's father . . ."

RUPERT TAKES COVER

The two chums hear a rustling sound
Which makes them start and turn around . . .

"There's someone there! Quick, follow me!
We'll try to hide behind a tree!"

The pals take cover. "This should do –
We'll see who else is coming too . . ."

"Look!" Rupert laughs. "All we could hear
Were just the footsteps of a deer!"

The two friends are still marvelling at the magic bottle when they suddenly hear a rustling sound from the bushes nearby. "W . . . what's that?" blinks Bill. "I think there's somebody coming!" whispers Rupert. "It might be the chamber's owner!" gasps his chum. "Quick, Rupert! We'd better hide." Dropping the bottle, the pair run off through the woods as fast as they can. "Take cover!" gasps Rupert. "We'll hide behind a stand of trees, then wait to see who's there . . ."

Turning off the forest path, the two chums plunge through the undergrowth then hide behind a tall tree, waiting to see who is coming . . . For a long time, all they can hear is the chirping of birds. Then, Bill hears the bushes stir again. "They're there!" he hisses. "Creeping up on us, from the sound of it! Perhaps they saw me go in?" Rupert peers out anxiously, then suddenly starts to laugh. "It's a deer!" he chuckles. "That's what we could hear! Fancy running away . . ."

RUPERT FINDS THE WAY

The chums have wandered off the track
And don't know which way to get back . . .

"There's only one way we can see!
I'll climb to the top of a tree . . ."

"The Professor's tower! Now I know
Exactly where we need to go . . ."

The pals spot Bodkin. "Hey!" they cry.
"We've found a hide-out, just nearby . . ."

Relieved that their fears were unfounded, Rupert and Bill head back through the forest towards the hollow tree. "We must be nearly there now," calls Bill. "I can't see it anywhere!" says Rupert. "In fact, I'm not even sure we're on the right path!" "You mean we're lost?" blinks his chum. "I'm afraid so!" nods Rupert. "We must have taken a wrong turn." Searching all round, he finally decides to climb to the top of a tree and look for familiar landmarks. "All we need is a pointer in the right direction . . ."

Climbing to the top of the tree, Rupert gazes out over a leafy canopy to the very edge of the woods. "I can see the Professor's tower from here!" he calls excitedly to Bill. "We're not that far away. I know which direction it's in now, so we won't get lost again . . ." Sure enough, the pals soon reach the far side of the forest where the distinctive building can be seen across the fields. "There's Bodkin!" says Rupert. "Let's go and tell him what we've discovered . . ."

RUPERT TALKS TO BODKIN

"I've never heard of it before!
Perhaps the Professor knows more . . ."

"He's gone away for days, but when
He gets back home, I'll tell him then . . ."

Next morning, Bill is keen to look
Again. "I know the path we took . . ."

"There's Farmer Brown! I wonder where
He's taking all those sheep up there?"

When Bodkin hears the pals' story, he shakes his head. "You find all sorts of things in those woods!" he says. "It's one of the oldest parts of the forest. The Professor might know something about it, but I'm afraid he's away at the moment. Won't be back for days . . ." Giving the chums a drink of lemonade, he waves goodbye as the pair set off along the path home. "Sorry I can't be more helpful," he smiles. "An underground hide-out's quite a find. It's probably been there for years and years . . ."

Next morning, Bill calls at Rupert's house to suggest going back to the woods to look for the chamber again. "I've been thinking about whose hide-out it was!" he says. "A hermit, perhaps? Living there, all alone." "Or an outlaw!" says Rupert. "Someone like Robin Hood. On the run from the King's men." The two pals are still on their way to the forest when they see Farmer Brown, driving a flock of sheep. "He's moving them out of the lower field," says Bill. "I wonder why?"

RUPERT HEARS ABOUT A FLOOD

"The low field's flooded! It's too deep
For cows to stay, never mind sheep!"

"A proper flood, and no mistake!
The river's spread out, like a lake!"

The pals walk on, along the "shore"
Then head into the woods once more . . .

"We need to find the hollow tree!
The trouble is, it's hard to see . . ."

Farmer Brown explains that he is having to move his sheep because the lower fields are all flooded. "The river must have burst its banks!" he says. "I don't know how, exactly. I didn't hear it rain in the night and everything was fine down there yesterday." "It looks like a pond!" says Bill. "Two fields completely submerged!" nods the farmer. "I've never known anything like it! Lucky I came by when I did or all the sheep would have had to swim to safety . . ."

Leaving the farmer to tend his flock, Rupert and Bill go down to the flooded fields to take a closer look. "It's funny the river should suddenly flood, like that!" says Rupert. "I suppose it must have worn away the bank." The pair continue on their way, towards the woods where they found the secret chamber. "It was somewhere near here, I'm sure!" says Bill. "The hollow tree is what we need to find. I can't remember the exact direction, but I think we came this way . . ."

RUPERT SEES THE FLOOD SPREAD

No matter how they search, the pair
Can't find the hide-out anywhere . . .

"The water's rising!" Rupert thinks.
"The flood has got much worse!" he blinks.

In Nutwood, Growler has a plan
To stop the water, if he can . . .

"This flood's something I can't explain!
Haven't had a drop of rain . . ."

No matter how hard Rupert and Bill search the forest, they still can't see the hollow tree . . . "Perhaps it's magic!" shrugs Bill. "That might explain why no-one has found the hidden chamber before." "Perhaps," says Rupert. "But I think it's more likely we're just looking in the wrong place." Eventually, the pals decide to give up and go home. On the way back, they see that the flooding from the river has got even worse. "Goodness!" blinks Rupert. "The water-level's rising fast!"

As the two pals reach the outskirts of Nutwood, they are surprised to find P.C. Growler preparing a thick wall of sandbags. "Can't be too careful!" he says. "If the water-level keeps on rising at this rate, the whole village could be flooded . . ." "It's happened before!" nods Gaffer Jarge. "I was a nipper at the time. It had been raining for ages then, though. Not like today. I can't understand it. Rivers don't just go flooding without any cause. 'Taint natural!"

RUPERT'S HOUSE IS CUT OFF

*"The newspaper says that there might
Be further flooding in the night . . ."*

*"This old barometer of mine
Says that the forecast's dry and fine!"*

*Next day, the sun is shining bright –
"The old barometer was right!"*

*But, looking out, Rupert sees how
The whole of Nutwood's flooded now . . .*

When Rupert arrives home he finds his parents are also worrying about the flooding . . . "The newspaper says it might reach the village tomorrow!" says Mrs. Bear. "There's a picture of Gaffer Jarge with a piece of seaweed. He claims it can predict the weather." "I'd rather trust my barometer!" laughs Mr. Bear. As Rupert goes to bed that night he checks the dial for a final reading. "High pressure! Sunny and dry!" he announces. "No danger of flooding then. We can all sleep safely . . ."

Next day, Rupert wakes to a bright, sunny morning. "Dad's barometer was right!" he smiles. "No rain today . . ." When he peers out of the window, he can hardly believe his eyes. "The whole garden's flooded!" he blinks. All Rupert can see is the very tops of the trees. "The water's even reached the downstairs windows!" he gasps. "We're cut off, like an island. I wonder what will happen next? If the flooding gets any worse, we'll have to climb on to the roof and wait to be rescued!"

RUPERT IS RESCUED BY HIS CHUM

"It's terrible!" says Mr. Bear.
"The flooding has spread everywhere!"

"Ahoy, there!" Bill calls. "I thought you
Might like to go exploring too . . ."

"Be careful, Rupert. Try to find
Dry land, if any's left behind . . ."

"The magic bottle that I dropped
Will pour out water till it's stopped!"

Rupert's parents are astonished by the flooding too. "It's extraordinary!" says Mr. Bear. "The whole village is under water. I've telephoned P.C. Growler and he's trying to get a motor launch from Nutchester to come and collect us all." Just then, Rupert hears a familiar voice calling his name. "It's Bill!" he cries. "He's got a rubber dingy." "Ahoy, there!" calls Rupert's chum. "I found this in our attic. It's from a trip to the seaside. Not very big, I'm afraid. But I think there's room for two . . ."

Rupert clambers out of the window and joins his chum in the dingy. "Do be careful!" calls Mrs. Bear. "Don't worry!" says Bill. "We'll head for high ground and look for help there . . ." As they row away from the stranded cottage, Bill reaches into his pocket and takes out a small, silver stopper. "I think I know what might have caused all this!" he says. "It must be that strange bottle we found and I dropped. If it really is magic, it might go on emptying out more and more water forever!"

RUPERT AND BILL LOOK FOR HELP

The Old Professor! Perhaps he
Is back by now? Let's go and see . . ."

Bodkin is safe but can't say when
His master will return again . . .

"There's one more person we might try –
His hilltop castle's quite nearby . . ."

"The Wise Old Goat! Let's ask him now –
We've got to stop the flood somehow . . ."

Who can the chums ask for help? "The Professor!" says Rupert. "Let's go and see if he's back." When the pair reach the Professor's tower, they find it surrounded by water, like a castle moat. "Isn't this terrible?" calls Bodkin. "The Professor's laboratory hasn't been flooded yet but the water's still rising!" "When do you expect him back?" calls Bill. "Next week, I think," says Bodkin. "He's gone to the South Seas to look at shells. I can't get in touch, I'm afraid. It's too far away . . ."

As the pals leave the Professor's tower they spot a little island in the distance. "It's the Wise Old Goat's castle!" says Rupert. "He must have been cut off too." The pair decide to ask the Goat's advice. "He might know something about stopping spells," says Bill. "He often makes charms and potions from herbs and wild berries." "It's worth a try," says Rupert. "I hope he's at home." "We'll soon find out," says Bill as they approach the castle. "I can't see anyone from here . . ."

RUPERT SEES THE WISE OLD GOAT

The two chums pull their boat ashore
Then climb up to the castle door . . .

They ask the Goat, "Please help us halt
The Nutwood flood. It's all our fault . . ."

"Remarkable!" the Wise Goat cries.
"That stopper's one I recognise!"

"I've seen it in an ancient book
On alchemy. Let's have a look . . ."

Landing on the little island, Rupert and Bill clamber to the top of the hill where the Wise Old Goat's castle stands. Ringing the bell, they wait for the door to open . . . "Rupert!" cries the castle's owner. "How nice to see you. I've been thinking about Nutwood all morning. Terrible flooding from what I can gather . . ." "That's right!" says Rupert. "We've come to ask your help." "To stop the water from rising any further?" asks the Goat. "That all depends on how it started . . ."

"Gracious me!" exclaims the Goat as the chums tell him the story of how they came across a secret chamber in the woods. "And that's the stopper from the magic bottle you found?" he asks. "It looks strangely familiar. From a drawing, I think . . ." Going to the bookcase, he reaches down a heavy, leather-bound volume. "Experiments in Alchemy!" he announces. "Written by one of my ancestors. I'm sure there's something about a flask with a silver stopper in here . . ."

Rupert and the Water Bottle

RUPERT LEARNS ABOUT THE BOTTLE

"Identical! The flask you found
Was a drought bottle, I'll be bound . . ."

"The magic only ceases when
The stopper's back in place again . . ."

The Wise Old Goat soon has a plan
To help the two chums, if he can . . .

"We need to reach the place where you
First found the bottle. That should do . . ."

"That's it!" gasps Bill as the Wise Old Goat leafs through the pages of a book. "A drought bottle!" nods the Goat. "One of my ancestor's finest inventions. It was his old workshop you tumbled into, no doubt. The bottle was meant to be a source of water in times of emergency. Harmless when stoppered but otherwise releasing unlimited quantities. Powerful magic's at work here, I fear. Unless we replace the stopper soon the whole of Nutwood will be completely submerged!"

"We must retrieve the bottle!" declares the Wise Old Goat. Taking a strange box from his desk, he also produces a butterfly net and several lengths of pole. "Launch your dingy!" he calls to Bill. "I'll sit at one end, while you and Rupert row . . ." Directing the pals back towards Nutwood, the Old Goat tells them to aim for the woods where they first found the hollow oak. "The treetops are still visible," he says. "The bottle must be underwater, somewhere down below . . ."

RUPERT GOES FISHING

"The viewing box light's glowing red
That means we're now right overhead . . ."

"Rupert! Start lowering the net
Reach down as far as you can get . . ."

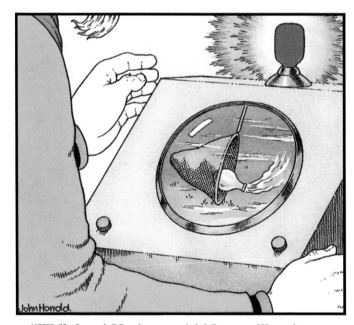

"I see the bottle! Nearly there . . ."
The two chums hear the Goat declare.

"Well done! You've got it! Now we'll see!
Bring up the net, please, carefully . . ."

When they reach the submerged wood, the Wise Old Goat tells Rupert and Bill to stop rowing and sit perfectly still. Pressing a button on the strange box, he lets the boat drift until a large red light begins to flash. "We're directly overhead!" he declares. "The viewing box has found the bottle, all we have to do now is catch it . . ." Handing Rupert the net, he tells him to lower it slowly over the side, extending the handle length by length, until he reaches the bottom of the lake . . .

As Bill and Rupert lower the net, the Wise Old Goat carefully watches a circular screen on the front of his box . . . "That's it!" he calls. "You're getting closer and closer. I can see the bottle perfectly clearly now." A moment later, the net itself appears on the screen, gliding slowly through the water towards the bottle. "Left a little!" calls the goat. "Now to the right. Well done, lads. You've got it! Bring the net up gently and we'll be able to have a good look at what we've caught . . ."

RUPERT FINDS THE MAGIC BOTTLE

"We've done it! Bravo!" both chums shout
As Rupert lifts the bottle out.

"Quick, put the cork in! That's the way!
You've stopped the water now! Hurray!"

"The flood's still here, but I think we
Can rectify that magically . . ."

"Wait here!" the Goat says. "While I look
At spells in my ancestor's book . . ."

When Rupert and Bill lift the net from the water they can see the magic bottle, still gushing water like an open tap . . . "Bravo!" calls the Wise Old Goat as the pair land their catch. "Now, Bill, get ready to stop it with the cork!" Lifting the bottle from the net, Rupert holds it steady while his chum pushes back the silver stopper. "That should do the trick!" says the Goat. "Now we have to find a way to get rid of all the flood water so that Nutwood gradually returns to normal . . ."

Although Rupert and Bill are glad to have stopped water pouring from the magic bottle, they are still mystified as to how the Wise Old Goat plans to clear up Nutwood's flood . . . "It's like a huge lake!" says Bill as they row back to the castle. "There's nowhere for the water to go . . ." "You'll see!" laughs the Goat. "My ancestor's invention caused all this. I think he can help us put things right as well. You two wait there, while I go inside and fetch his book of spells . . ."

RUPERT HELPS TO CAST A SPELL

"I thought I saw a counter charm!
It should soon clear up any harm . . ."

"Reverse the spell and help restore
All Nutwood as it was before . . ."

A gentle wind begins to blow
Then, gradually, it starts to grow . . .

'A hurricane! We'd better hide!
Quick, everybody. Get inside!"

The Wise Old Goat emerges from the castle with his ancestor's book and a long, wooden staff. "I thought so!" he smiles. "We can reverse the spell with a counter charm. Rupert, you keep the bottle safe, while Bill holds the book . . ." Reading aloud from the spell to cure droughts, the Goat strikes the ground with his staff and recites another rhyme. "Reverse the spell and take away the flood you caused, without delay. Let Nutwood's fields appear once more and all be as it was before . . ."

As he finishes speaking, the Wise Old Goat stands still as a statue, staring out intently across the flooded fields. At first, nothing seems to happen. Then a wind starts to ruffle the surface of the water, blowing stronger and stronger. The sky grows dark and a huge, swirling cloud appears . . . "It's a tornado!" cries Bill. "You're right!" calls the Goat. "We'd better take shelter inside. It's only just starting. I think we're going to be right in the eye of the storm . . ."

RUPERT SEES A WHIRLWIND

As the whirlwind spins far and near
The flood begins to disappear . . .

It moves towards the castle, where
It spins, like a top, in mid-air.

The Goat tells Rupert he must hold
The bottle ready when he's told . . .

"Remove the cork and wait until
The whirlwind gets here. Just keep still . . ."

From inside the Old Goat's castle, Rupert and Bill watch the whirlwind swirl and spin over the countryside around Nutwood. "It's sucking up water!" cries Rupert. "Reversing the spell!" nods the Wise Old Goat. "You can see the cloud above growing fuller and fuller . . ." As the waters clear, the tornado wheels towards the castle, like a giant spinning top. "Up the stairs to the top of the round tower!" calls the Goat. "And don't forget to bring the bottle . . ."

As they reach the top of the tower, the chums can see the whirlwind approaching . . . "It's coming straight at us!" blinks Bill. "Exactly!" says the Goat. "We're in just the right place . . ." Telling Rupert to take the stopper from the bottle, he gets him to hold it out at arm's length. "Keep it steady and don't move!" he calls. "You'll be perfectly safe, so long as you do exactly as I say!" Removing the cork, Rupert stands ready and waits for the cyclone to arrive . . .

RUPERT ENDS THE STORM

The whirlwind stops where Rupert stands
Then follows the Wise Goat's commands . . .

"It's nearly gone! The end's in sight!
Quick, Rupert! Put the cork in tight . . ."

"Well done, the bottle's full once more
And Nutwood's as it was before . . ."

"I'm glad the flood has gone but, still,
It was quite fun as well," says Bill.

The sound of the wind grows louder and louder. As Rupert holds the bottle out, the whole swirling mass sinks down in the sky until it is only inches away from his outstretched arm. "The time for Nutwood's flood has ceased!" commands the Wise Old Goat. "Draw back the water you released . . ." To Rupert's amazement, the tail of the whirlwind sinks into the bottle, like a huge genie returning to its lamp. "Nearly done!" laughs the Goat. "Now get ready with the cork . . ."

As the last of the whirlwind vanishes inside the bottle, Rupert pushes home the stopper with a cry of triumph. "Well done, you two!" says the Wise Old Goat. "We won't be troubled by that again!" Taking the bottle from Rupert, he puts it safely away in a cupboard while the chums have a well-earned snack. "What an adventure!" says Rupert. "Magic!" laughs Bill. "Although I think it will be quite a while before I try climbing inside any more hollow trees . . ."

Where is Gregory?

Gregory Guinea-pig has disappeared.
Look carefully at the hopscotch squares to see where he has gone.

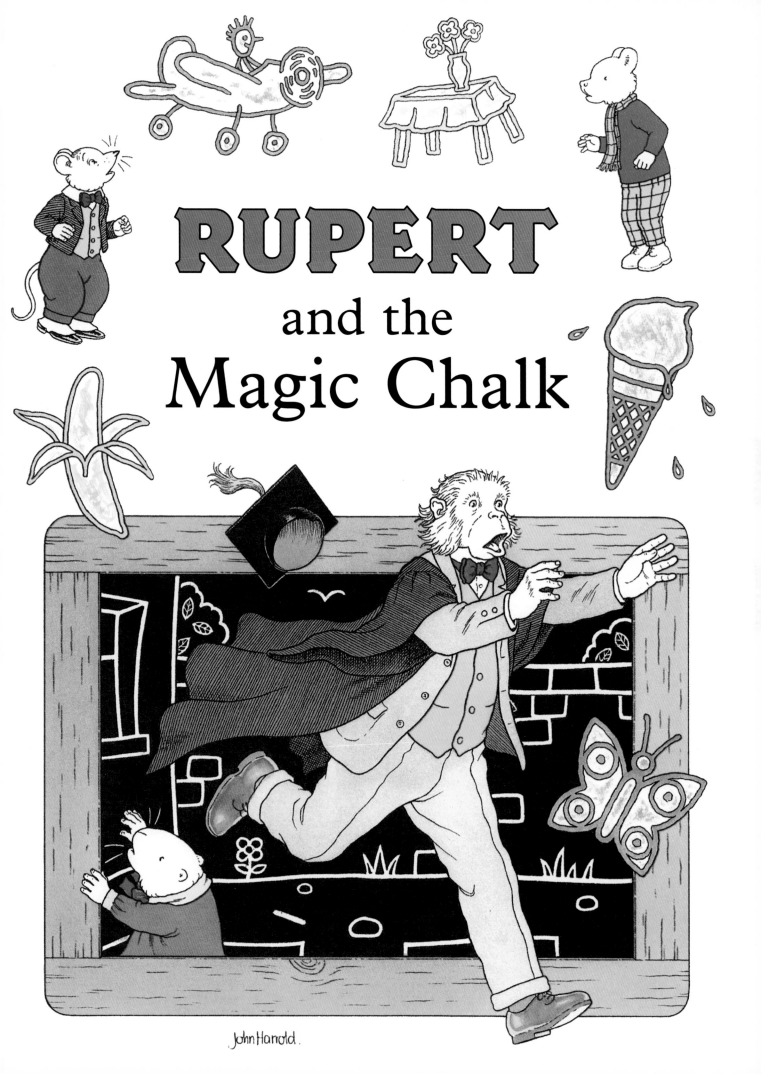

RUPERT
and the
Magic Chalk

John Harrold.

RUPERT GOES BACK TO SCHOOL

Today is the first morning when
The Nutwood chums start school again.

Their teacher says he hopes that they
Enjoyed the summer holiday.

This morning there's a treat in store –
"I'll get some chalk and you can draw . . ."

"Please pass the box round and . . . Oh, dear!
We've run out! There's none left in here!"

The summer holidays are over and it is the start of a new school term for Rupert and his friends. "Hello, Bill!" calls Rupert as he hurries on his way. "Everyone is very punctual this morning! I can see Bingo, the Rabbit twins, and even Podgy's arriving on time!" The playground is full of excited chums, all catching up with each other's news. "Hello, everyone!" beams Dr Chimp as he comes out to ring the bell. "I hope you had a good summer! It's nice to see you all again . . ."

"Welcome back to school!" says Dr Chimp. "We'll start the new term with some drawing practice. I don't mind what you decide to draw, so long as you make a good job of it!" As the pals take out their slates, he rummages behind his desk and produces a large cardboard box. "Chalk!" he smiles. "You can pass it round and each take a stick . . ." As he opens the box, Dr Chimp's smile fades. "Oh, dear!" he blinks. "It's all gone! We must have run out at the end of last term!"

The guinea-pig calls, "Hop, jump, hop!
It's easy – but you mustn't stop!"

Then, suddenly, the ground gives way –
The pals look on in shocked dismay!

A trap door snaps shut instantly,
Leaving no sign of Gregory . . .

"Fetch Dr Chimp!" calls Rupert, then
Gasps in amazement once again . . .

Laying his chalk to one side, Gregory stands in the first square, ready to start the game. "Hop, jump, hop, jump, hop, jump!" he calls. "Your feet mustn't touch the lines and you have to keep moving . . ." Suddenly, the guinea-pig's glee gives way to a cry of dismay as a trap door swings open and sends him plummeting into a gloomy pit. "What's happening?" blinks Freddy. "There wasn't a door there a moment ago!" "I know!" says Rupert and runs forward to see what's become of his chum.

To Rupert's astonishment, the mysterious door swings shut again as suddenly as it opened . . . "Gregory!" he calls. "Are you all right?" "He's shut in!" gasps Freddy. "The squares fit so snugly you can't even see a gap!" "We'll have to fetch Dr Chimp!" says Rupert, but at that very moment, their teacher comes sprinting into the playground, running as fast as he can. "I wonder what's wrong?" blinks Bill. "It almost looks as though something is chasing him . . ."

RUPERT'S TEACHER IS AMAZED

"A dinosaur!" the teacher cries,
Unable to believe his eyes!

"They're all our drawings!" Rupert blinks.
"Each one has come to life!" he thinks.

"Oh, no!" says Tigerlily. "My
Chalk must be magic – that is why!"

The strange procession carries on,
Then Dr Chimp spots where it's gone!

"Look out!" warns Dr Chimp. "There's a dinosaur on the loose!" "A dinosaur?" gasps Rupert. "Why, it's Ottoline's Triceratops!" "Keep back!" warns his teacher as the huge creature lumbers into the playground. "But how has my drawing come to life?" asks Ottoline. "And why has it grown so big?" Before anyone can answer, a strange procession comes following in the dinosaur's wake . . . "My rocket!" marvels Rupert. "All the drawings have come to life!"

As Dr Chimp and his pupils stand gazing at the astonishing parade, Tigerlily picks up Gregory's stick of chalk and gives a cry of dismay. "It must be magic! My father always has some that he uses for conjuring tricks. The packets in his study must have got muddled up – he's given me the wrong one!" More and more chalk creations emerge from the classroom and file past Dr Chimp. "They're escaping into Nutwood!" he gasps. "Goodness knows what they'll get up to there!"

RUPERT FOLLOWS A DINOSAUR

"They're bound for Nutwood High Street now,
We've got to stop them all somehow!"

"'Tis fancy dress!" old Gaffer jeers
As the bizarre parade appears.

When Growler sees the dinosaur
He says that it's breaking the law!

The creature knocks him off his feet,
Then lumbers on along the street . . .

Rupert and Dr Chimp run out of the school gates and after the runaway drawings. "Come back!" calls the teacher but the strange procession pays no heed . . . Nutwood's inhabitants blink in amazement as the chalk creatures reach the High Street. "A fancy dress parade!" says Gaffer Jarge. "The things they get up to these days! When I was a lad, we spent all day in the classroom." "I don't think it's fancy dress," murmurs Mrs. Sheep. "The dinosaur's so heavy it's making the ground shake!"

Rupert and Bill run on ahead of the others until they reach the start of the procession. P.C. Growler has already spotted the commotion and orders the Triceratops to stop. "Halt, in the name of the Law!" he shouts, blocking the creature's path. The dinosaur pauses, then lowers its head and nudges Growler aside. "Now, then!" he warns. "Any of that and I'll place you under arrest!" The dinosaur lumbers forward and catches Growler with its tail, sending him sprawling . . .

RUPERT THINKS OF A PLAN

He isn't hurt but says the beast
Deserves to be locked up, at least!

"Come on, Bill. Perhaps you and I
Can stop them all. We've got to try!"

Then Rupert has a good idea –
"I've got some magic chalk left here!"

"We'll head them off this way!" he cries.
"I want to take them by surprise . . ."

A startled shopkeeper hurries forward to help P.C. Growler to his feet. "Are you all right?" he gasps. "Yes, thanks," murmurs the dazed policeman, "but if I ever catch that dinosaur I'll lock it up for disturbing the peace!" Before he can say any more, Rupert and Bill hurry away in pursuit of the unruly procession . . . "We've got to do something to stop them!" calls Bill. "If the Triceratops gets as far as Nutchester, it will cause havoc! The town could come to a standstill!"

As the chums chase after the runaway creatures, Rupert suddenly has a good idea. "The chalk!" he cries. "Tigerlily gave me Gregory's stick to look after when we were standing in the playground. I think I know how we can use it to sort things out . . ." Beckoning for Bill to follow, he leaves the path and sets off across the fields as fast as he can go. "We need to get far enough ahead of the procession to prepare a surprise!" he calls. "If they see what I'm up to, the plan won't work."

RUPERT DRAWS A DOOR

The two pals reach the road once more.
"That wall's the perfect place to draw!"

"Another drawing?" Bill can't see
What use the magic chalk will be . . .

"Look out!" he calls. "They're on their way.
It isn't safe for us to stay!"

But then, the door that Rupert drew
Swings open and they all march through!

Cutting across the field, Rupert joins the road again as it nears a steep bank. "Perfect!" he cries. "There will just be time to make another drawing before the chalk creatures arrive . . ." "Another drawing?" blinks Bill. "I thought we had enough already!" "This one's different!" says Rupert. He draws a long straight line as high as he can, then gets Bill to lift him on to his shoulders. "It's like drawing the goalposts for a game of football in the playground!" says Bill.

When he has finished drawing on the wall, Rupert takes the chalk and marks a pathway on the road. "Quick!" calls Bill. "The procession's nearly here." As Rupert hurries over to join him, the Triceratops lumbers along the path towards the wall. To Bill's astonishment a great door swings open, revealing a long, dark tunnel. "Magic chalk!" laughs Rupert. "Magic brought the creatures into Nutwood and this way it will take them out again . . ."

"How odd!" says Dr Chimp. "I'm sure
That tunnel wasn't here before!"

As Bill explains, the pals decide
To see if Gregory's inside.

"I'm coming with you!" Bill calls. "Wait!"
But then the door shuts. It's too late!

Inside the tunnel there's no light,
"It's like the middle of the night!"

Dr Chimp is astonished to see the chalk creatures disappearing into a secret chamber. "I didn't know there was a door here!" he blinks. "There wasn't until a few moments ago!" says Bill and explains how Rupert drew it with Tigerlily's chalk. Willie Mouse joins Rupert as the last creatures enter the tunnel. "Where are they going?" he blinks. "I'm not sure," admits Rupert. "But I'm certain it's where we'll find Gregory. All we have to do is follow the procession . . ."

Rupert and Willie follow the chalk creatures into the tunnel only to find the door swinging shut behind them . . . "Wait for me!" calls Bill, but it's too late. As the door slams shut the pair are plunged into total darkness. All they can see is the outline of a chalk boomerang, spinning through the air. "Quick!" calls Rupert. "We mustn't let it out of sight!" Hurrying forward, they find themselves back in the procession, but with no idea where the path they're following might end.

The pals are left behind as they
Watch the procession speed away.

When Rupert follows it he sees
A chalk path, drawn through hills and trees . . .

"A shepherd! Let's ask if he knows
The way – and where this pathway goes!"

"Just carry on," he tells the pair.
"You'll soon reach Chalk Town – over there."

As Rupert and Willie follow the procession they find the tunnel growing wider and wider. "We've come out into a field!" blinks Rupert. The chalk creatures lumber on, then suddenly disappear over the brow of a hill . . . When Rupert and Willie follow, they are astonished to see a whole landscape of hills and trees. "Everything has been drawn in chalk!" cries Willie. "It's like being on a huge blackboard!" "I can see a road," says Rupert. "Let's take that and see where it leads . . ."

The two chums follow the road, which twists and turns through blackboard fields of sheep. After a while, they spot a shepherd and stop to ask directions. "Hello!" calls Rupert. "My friend and I were wondering if you can tell us where we are? We started by following a great procession but seem to have lost our way . . ." "I haven't seen any procession," says the shepherd. "But you're on the road to Chalk Town . . . Those houses mark the outskirts. Keep going and you can't miss it."

RUPERT VISITS CHALK TOWN

The two pals reach the town, then walk
Through streets of houses drawn with chalk . . .

"We're lost!" says Rupert. "I don't know
In which direction we should go!"

The streets seem empty, then, at last,
A boy walking his dog goes past . . .

They ask if he's seen Gregory –
"The Quarry's where he's bound to be!"

Rupert and Willie soon arrive in the middle of Chalk Town. "The houses look like drawings on a blackboard!" says Willie. "Yes!" laughs Rupert. "Everything here looks like a drawing. I suppose it's what you'd expect in the Land of Chalk . . ." As the pair get used to the strange surroundings, they look around for someone to ask about Gregory. "He's bound to be here somewhere!" says Willie. "I wonder?" murmurs Rupert. "So far, Chalk Town seems to be completely deserted!"

Although Chalk Town seems empty, the chums finally spot a young boy out walking his dog . . . "Hello!" calls Rupert. "We're looking for a friend of ours. I wonder if you've seen him . . ." The boy listens carefully to his description of Gregory then shakes his head. "I haven't seen anyone like that!" he says, "But he might be with the others, up at the Quarry . . ." "Quarry?" blinks Rupert. "Yes," says the boy. "Where they dig for chalk. Everyone in Chalk Town works there!"

RUPERT SEES A QUARRY

The chums set off without delay,
Then spot a sign which points the way.

"Look!" Rupert marvels. All around
Are men, digging chalk from the ground . . .

The pals explain that they have come
To try to find their missing chum.

"Try Processing! I think they had
A new recruit – an eager lad!

Following the boy's directions, Rupert and Willie set off along the road through Chalk Town and past a large sign which points to the quarry. Peering down, they are astonished to see a huge white gash in the hillside with teams of men chipping away at the rock . . . "It looks enormous!" gasps Rupert. "I wonder if Gregory is somewhere down there with them?" asks Willie. "I don't know," says Rupert. "Let's go and ask if anyone has seen him . . ."

Clambering down to the chalk face, Rupert and Willie look anxiously around for someone to ask about Gregory . . . "New recruits?" calls a man with a clipboard. "I expect you saw our advert for vacancies . . ." "Not exactly!" explains Rupert. "We were looking for a friend of ours who might have joined you earlier . . ." "From Chalk Town?" asks the man. "No," explains Rupert. "He lives with us in Nutwood . . ." "Try Processing," suggests the foreman. "That's where newcomers usually start."

RUPERT LOOKS FOR GREGORY

Inside the building the pair see
Chalk processing machinery . . .

"Hello!" calls Rupert. "Is it true
There's someone working here that's new?"

The first man sends the chums to where
The sticks of chalk are packed. "Try there . . ."

"A guinea-pig? Why, yes! I'm sure
He's working in the room next door . . ."

Inside the building, Rupert and Willie find workers from the quarry loading chalk boulders into a huge machine . . . A tremendous clanking sound fills the air as the rocks are pounded and pummelled into dust. The men are so busy that nobody notices the chums peeping round the door. "Hello!" shouts Rupert above the noise. "We've come to look for a friend of ours called Gregory . . ." "Try the Packing Department," suggests one of the men. "I think there's a new arrival working there."

Rupert and Willie walk towards the far end of the building, where the machine is pouring out hundreds of sticks of newly made chalk. As it tumbles down a chute, the chalk is packed into boxes. "Is this the Packing Department?" asks Rupert. "I've come to look for a friend of mine, called Gregory . . ." "The young guinea-pig who's just joined us!" smiles a man. "He's hard at work in the next building. Through that door and keep going. You're bound to see him straightaway . . ."

RUPERT FINDS HIS CHUM

"At last!" cries Rupert, glad they've found
Their missing schoolmate, safe and sound.

"Hello!" smiles Gregory. "What fun!
I'm sending chalk to everyone . . ."

"We can't stay in Chalk Town but how
Will we get back to Nutwood now?"

"That box says Nutwood!" Rupert blinks.
"There must be a way back . . ." he thinks.

As the door swings open, Rupert finally spots Gregory, sitting at a desk with a large pot of glue and a pile of labels. "Hello!" calls the little guinea-pig. "Isn't this fun! I've always wondered how chalk was made. First I had a guided tour of the Quarry and then they let me help in the Packing Department . . ." "What are you doing?" asks Willie. "Sticking address labels on all the boxes!" smiles Gregory. "You'd be amazed at the different places they go – all over the world!"

Rupert and Willie are glad that Gregory is safe but can't think how to go about leaving the Land of Chalk. "I was having such fun, I never thought about that!" admits Gregory. "There must be a way out," murmurs Rupert. "After all, we found a way in . . ." Looking round the factory, he suddenly stares at the pile of boxes. "Nutwood!" he cries. "Look, Gregory! One of the boxes is addressed to our village. All we have to do is find out how it's being sent!"

RUPERT LEADS THE WAY

A clerk says Dr Chimp is due
More chalk. "He's who we send it to . . ."

"You've run out? Then I think that we
Should use Express Delivery!"

"Wait there!" he says and starts to draw
The pals a tiny little door . . .

"You'll soon be there. It isn't far!"
He smiles and holds the door ajar.

Gregory tells his chums that the Clerk in charge of orders keeps them written down in a big, heavy book. "Nutwood?" he smiles when Rupert shows him the box of chalk. "That must be for Dr Chimp! He's one of our best customers. A regular order at the start of each term . . ." "But term has already started!" says Willie. "Dr Chimp's run out of chalk. That's why he borrowed some from Tigerlily!" "Run out?" cries the Clerk. "We'd better send this Express Delivery! Follow me . . ."

The Clerk leads the chums along a dark corridor, which has a little door at the far end. "Dr Chimp's orders normally go by post!" he says. "But as things are so urgent, I think you should deliver the chalk by hand . . ." Pulling the door open, he reveals a brightly lit room on the far side and invites the astonished pals to clamber through. "You won't have much further to go!" he promises. "Do send Dr Chimp our apologies. I'll make sure his order is never late again!"

RUPERT AND HIS PALS RETURN

The three chums are astonished when
They find they're back at school again!

"The door just vanished!" Willie cries.
He shakes his head and rubs his eyes.

"You're back!" gasps Dr Chimp. "I feared
The three of you had disappeared!"

The chums laugh as they show him how
He's got a box of new chalk now . . .

When Rupert and the others jump down, they are amazed to find themselves standing at the front of their classroom in Nutwood. "I told you it wasn't far!" laughs the Clerk. Rupert spins round towards the blackboard, but the little door has vanished as miraculously as it first appeared. "I don't believe it!" gasps Willie. "But we did all go to the Land of Chalk, didn't we?" says Gregory. "We certainly did!" nods Rupert. "And here's a box of chalk to prove it!"

The pals are still marvelling at their adventure when who should stride into the room but Dr Chimp. . . "Rupert! Willie!" he gasps. "You're back! And young Gregory too. Thank goodness for that! I was sure you had all disappeared forever!" "We went to the Land of Chalk!" cries Willie. "The Land of where?" blinks his teacher. "Chalk!" laughs Rupert. "They sent you this box by special delivery. Very special indeed . . ."

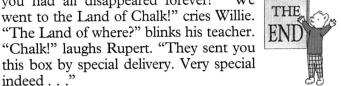

Mirror Land Chums

Rupert is surprised to see what his chums are wearing in Mirror Land.
Can you draw them in their usual clothes in the frame below?

RUPERT'S MAZE OF BUTTERFLIES

Start at the flower in the top left-hand corner and trace your way along the white paths until you reach the flower in the bottom right-hand corner. Only one of the paths will lead you there – the others are put in to puzzle you. When you have found the right path, hold the page at arm's length and you will soon see the shape of another butterfly in the white lines. You can then have the fun of shading the outline with your pencil to make the butterfly stand out boldly.

RUPERT and

One fine spring morning Rupert goes
In search of all the pals he knows.

One fine spring morning Rupert decides to go for a walk on Nutwood common. "I wonder if I'll meet anyone?" he thinks. "Bill and Algy might be playing football." As he carries on Rupert notices a little bird. It hovers above him for a moment then swoops down purposefully. To Rupert's surprise, it calls his name. "Thank goodness I've found you! Odmedod the scarecrow asked me to deliver an important message . . ."

the Goose Chase

A bird flies down. "Rupert! I've come
From Odmedod, your scarecrow chum . . ."

"What Odmedod told me to say,
Was, can you please come straightaway?"

The bird tells Rupert that Odmedod wants to see him. "Something strange has happened at the farm!" it explains. Rupert agrees to come at once. "Odmedod is in the far field," the bird chirps. "He couldn't come and find you himself in case anyone saw!" Rupert follows the bird across the fields towards Farmer Brown's. After a while he spots a familiar figure standing in the distance. "Good!" says the bird. "Nobody else is there."

The scarecrow stands upon a hill
He doesn't move but keeps quite still . . .

"Hello!" says Odmedod. "I knew
You'd come if I sent word to you . . ."

"I didn't want to cause alarm
But something's happened at the farm!"

"A stranger came and, so I'm told,
He spoke of goose eggs made from gold . . ."

"It sounds unlikely but those two
Seem quite convinced it might be true!"

Rupert hurries across the field to Odmedod. "Hello!" calls the scarecrow. "Sorry to bother you, but I've made a strange discovery I think you should know about . . ." To Rupert's astonishment, Odmedod looks all round then starts to whisper. "A stranger came to the farm a few days ago and was asking lots of questions about the geese!" "Geese?" blinks Rupert. "Yes," says Odmedod. "He thought that one of them was different from all the others. He claimed it could lay golden eggs!"

"A goose that lays golden eggs?" marvels Rupert. "It sounds like a fairy tale." "That's what I thought!" nods Odmedod. "The odd thing is, a new goose has arrived on the farm. Mollie and Mildred saw it crossing the yard." "Mollie?" asks Rupert. The scarecrow points to a pair of horses in the next field. "Their stables are near the farmhouse so they see everything that happens . . ." The horses tell Rupert that the new goose looks just like all the others but seems very shy.

RUPERT GOES TO THE FARM

"I'll go and see what I can find –
I'm sure that Farmer Brown won't mind . . ."

"Another visitor! I'm sure
I've never seen their car before . . ."

"Two men came earlier to see
If they could buy goose eggs from me . . ."

A sudden honking fills the air –
"That's Gertie! She might peck the pair!"

Intrigued by Odmedod's story, Rupert decides to go to the farm and see the new goose for himself. "I wonder if it really can lay golden eggs?" he thinks. "Mrs Brown will know if anyone does. I'll ask her if she's seen anything strange." As Rupert reaches the farm, he spots an odd-looking car parked in the courtyard. "I've never seen that before!" he blinks. "Perhaps it's one of the Professor's new inventions. I wonder if he has heard about the new goose too?"

When Rupert reaches the farmhouse he calls to ask Mrs Brown what has been happening. "It's all very odd!" she shrugs. "A man came to talk about geese the other day and now he's back, together with his servant. They want to buy a basket of eggs." Rupert is about to ask more when he hears a sudden commotion from the other side of the yard. "The geese!" gasps Mrs Brown. "They sound angry about something. I hope those men are safe. They'll get pecked if they upset Gertie."

RUPERT SEES HUMPHREY PUMPHREY

"Sir Humphrey Pumphrey!" Rupert blinks.
"He must be after gold!" he thinks . . .

"Don't worry! It's a false alarm.
The noisy geese have done no harm."

"Sir Humphrey's had no luck, I see . . .
I wonder what the truth can be?"

Rupert explores, intrigued to find
A single goose that's stayed behind.

As Rupert and Mrs Brown cross the farmyard, two men appear, pursued by angry geese! "Sir Humphrey Pumphrey!" gasps Rupert. "He must be the stranger the horses saw. I wonder if he's found any golden eggs?" "Goodness!" exclaims the farmer's wife. "I hope you haven't been injured! I must apologise for Gertie's behaviour." "No need to worry!" says Sir Humphrey. "Scrogg and I have got all the eggs we need. I expect the geese just aren't used to visitors."

Rupert watches thoughtfully as Humphrey Pumphrey goes back to his car. "I'm sure he's after the goose that lays golden eggs!" he thinks. "I expect he wants to put it in his private zoo . . ." Still not sure what to make of Odmedod's story, he decides to take a closer look in the goose-hut. At first Rupert thinks the geese have all gone, but, as he steps inside, he suddenly spots one hiding in the straw. "Don't worry!" he whispers. "I won't give you away . . ."

RUPERT MEETS A SPECIAL GOOSE

The goose looks up. "No need to fear,
But I know why you're hiding here . . ."

"Hello!" says Gertie. "Don't say you
Have come to look for goose eggs too?"

"A golden egg! It's really true!
No wonder Pumphrey's after you . . ."

"He's not the only one, you know!
Men chase me everywhere I go!"

Although the goose looks just like all the others, Rupert feels certain it is the one Sir Humphrey has been looking for . . . "Odmedod the scarecrow told me all about you," he explains. "I didn't believe him at first, but now I think the stories must be true . . ." As Rupert speaks, Gertie and the other geese come waddling back, still laughing at the way they saw off Scrogg and Sir Humphrey. "Rupert!" she blinks. "What are you doing here? Don't say you've come looking for eggs as well!"

Rupert tells the geese he has come to warn them about Sir Humphrey and his zoo. "Thank you!" sighs the golden goose. "Everywhere I go, people are after me. Always for the same reason . . ." Pointing to a nest in the straw she shows Rupert a gleaming gold egg. "We've done what we can to help," says Gertie. "But I don't think we've seen the last of Sir Humphrey Pumphrey!" "You're right!" nods Rupert. "We'll have to make a plan in case he comes back . . ."

RUPERT IS WORRIED

The farmyard geese tell Rupert how
They'll all be on the look-out now . . .

"Sir Humphrey and his friend just paid
For every egg our geese had laid!"

"There must be something I can do
To save the goose from Pumphrey's zoo . . ."

As Rupert wanders home he hears
A call. The Sage of Um appears!

Rupert promises the geese that he will come back and see them again as soon as he has thought of a plan. "In the meanwhile we'll all keep a look-out!" says Gertie. "If anyone spots Sir Humphrey they'll raise the alarm by honking as loud as they can." Mrs Brown tells Rupert that the visitors bought a whole basket of eggs and said they might be back later in the week for more. "I can't understand why they want so many!" she exclaims. "One goose egg is just like another!"

As Rupert walks back from the farm, he thinks of how Sir Humphrey Pumphrey will stop at nothing to get what he wants . . . "There must be something I can do to help the golden goose!" he sighs. "It isn't safe for it to stay on the farm." Just then, Rupert hears a cheery call and looks up to see the Sage of Um, in his flying Brella. "Hello!" cries the visitor. "I was just on my way home from Nutwood when I suddenly spotted you walking along. Wait there and I'll come down for a chat."

RUPERT'S FRIEND HAS AN IDEA

The Sage of Um says, "Tell me why
You looked perplexed as I flew by . . ."

He hears about the golden goose –
And how Sir Humphrey's on the loose!

"I know! The golden goose can come
And live in peace with me, on Um . . . !"

"We'll go and let your parents know –
I'm sure they won't mind if you go."

The Sage of Um is a wise old man who lives on a faraway island, together with the last herd of unicorns in the world. He has often helped Rupert before and listens carefully to his story about the goose and Sir Humphrey Pumphrey . . . "Such a creature would be a great prize!" he frowns. "You're right to be concerned. Sir Humphrey will keep searching, especially if he thinks the other geese have something to hide. We need to think of somewhere else for the goose to stay!"

Rupert and the Sage think hard for a moment, then both come up with the same answer . . . "Um Island!" laughs Rupert's friend. "The goose will be safe from Sir Humphrey there. Hardly anyone knows where to find Um and it never appears on maps." The Sage suggests that Rupert should tell the goose their plan and accompany it on the journey. "First, we must go and ask your parents," he declares. "I'm sure they won't mind when they hear why you want to go . . ."

"Yes," Mrs Bear smiles. "I agree!
But only if you stay for tea . . ."

The pair set out, but as they go
The sun sets with an orange glow.

"I'll wait here," says the Sage. "Look out!
There may be people still about . . ."

Rupert creeps forward silently.
"Hello!" he says. "It's only me!"

Mr and Mrs Bear are pleased to see the Sage and happily agree to Rupert visiting Um Island. "I hope you'll stay for tea before you go!" says Rupert's mother. "I want to hear all about the unicorns . . ." The sky is darkening by the time Rupert and his friend set out for Farmer Brown's, but the Sage seems unconcerned. "It's probably as well for the goose to stay out of sight during the day," he declares. "Sir Humphrey might be keeping watch! We don't want him to see us arrive."

As the pair near the farm, the Sage tells Rupert he will wait for him outside. "The less disturbance we make the better!" he declares. "Bring the golden goose back with you and we'll be able to take off in the Brella without being seen." Rupert crosses the silent farmyard and tiptoes to the hut where the geese all live. "Hello!" he whispers. "It's me, Rupert Bear! I've thought of somewhere safe for you to go. Come out and join me. We can set off while it's dark, so that nobody sees . . ."

RUPERT IS CAUGHT

"I've come to take you far away
To somewhere where it's safe to stay!"

The goose agrees. "I thought those men
Might come and search the farm again . . ."

Scrogg blocks the way. "You don't fool me!
Is that a golden egg I see?"

He grabs the goose, and Rupert too,
"Sir Humphrey wants a word with you!"

The golden goose is delighted with Rupert's plan. "Um Island sounds perfect!" it smiles. "Peace and quiet, no nosy visitors and with all those unicorns for company I'll certainly never be lonely!" Disappearing into the goose hut to say its farewells, it emerges with the golden egg and follows Rupert across the farmyard, to where the Sage is waiting . . . "I was so worried those men might come back!" the goose tells Rupert. "They didn't seem the type to give up easily!"

"Give up?" growls a deep voice. "Just as well we didn't, isn't it? Sir Humphrey said we'd find you sooner or later, and here you are – with a golden egg too! He will be pleased . . ." Before Rupert can stop him, the burly figure picks up the goose and calls to his companion. "Bring the bear as well!" orders Sir Humphrey. "We don't want him running off for help as soon as we're gone." Seizing Rupert by his jumper, Scrogg lifts him up and strides towards the waiting car.

The path's blocked by an angry flock
Of geese, which give Scrogg quite a shock!

"Quick!" Rupert urges. "Run while they
Stop Scrogg and let us get away!"

The Sage spots Rupert. "Goodness me!
We need to leave immediately . . ."

He hovers ready in mid-air,
"I'll save you from that pesky pair!"

Just as it seems that all is lost, a noisy honking sound makes Scrogg stop in his tracks. The next moment, Gertie and the other geese crowd around him, hissing and pecking angrily. "Stop that! Help!" cries Sir Humphrey's servant, flailing at the birds in alarm. "Come on!" Rupert whispers to the golden goose. "Now's our chance! Your friends will give us time to get away." "Scrogg!" calls Sir Humphrey. "Leave those silly geese and get after the one with the golden egg!"

"Come back here!" bellows Scrogg. "You won't get away that easily, you know!" By now Rupert has spotted the Sage of Um, who blinks with surprise, then hops into the waiting Brella. By the time Rupert reaches him, his friend is hovering in the air, poised for a quick escape . . . "Well done!" he calls. "Jump aboard and you'll soon be out of Sir Humphrey's reach." Rupert seizes his hand and clambers in. The goose follows, leaping into Rupert's arms as the Brella starts to rise.

RUPERT FLIES IN THE BRELLA

Scrogg tries to catch the goose but fails –
"They're flying out of reach!" he wails.

Sir Humphrey shakes his fist. "I'll get
That goose in my collection yet!"

"Don't worry! He won't capture you
And put you in a private zoo . . ."

"Look out!" cries Rupert. "Down below,
They're following us as we go!"

Scrogg makes a desperate lunge as the Brella takes off but it is too late . . . "Hold on tight!" calls the Sage. "Up we go!" Rupert and the goose peer down at Sir Humphrey and Scrogg, who stand gasping in the farmyard below. "Hurrah!" laughs Rupert. "We made it! You'll be safe now." "Don't be so sure!" calls Sir Humphrey, shaking his fist angrily. "Nobody makes a fool of me and gets away with it. I'll catch that goose if it's the last thing I do! Just you wait and see . . ."

"Sir Humphrey Pumphrey!" scoffs the Sage as the Brella flies away from Nutwood. "People like that are a real menace. The very thought of putting our friend here in a private zoo! I'm glad to say there's no danger of that happening now. He'll never find you on Um, no matter how much he huffs and puffs." Rupert looks back towards the farm and spots a fast car speeding along the road. "It's Sir Humphrey and Scrogg!" he gasps. "They must have decided to follow us . . ."

RUPERT IS FOLLOWED

The Sage tells Rupert not to mind.
"We'll soon leave Pumphrey far behind!"

"Sir Humphrey has to stop, while we
Can fly on, out across the sea."

The car drives straight towards the shore
But just as quickly as before!

"Bless me!" the Sage blinks. "It can float –
Sir Humphrey's car's just like a boat!"

Although Sir Humphrey's car is very fast, the Sage of Um doesn't seem to be too bothered by the thought of being chased . . . "Look!" he laughs and points ahead. "The sea!" cries Rupert. "Of course! He won't be able to follow us now." "That's one of the main reasons I settled on Um!" says the Sage. "It's miles and miles from the mainland." They reach the coast and sail out across the sea, which glistens in the silvery moonlight. "Full speed ahead!" calls the Sage.

As the Brella flies out to sea, Rupert looks back towards Sir Humphrey. "He's still driving fast!" he calls. "They'll end up in the sea if they don't stop soon!" blinks the Sage. To the friends' astonishment, their pursuer shows no sign of slowing down but drives straight towards them, floating on the surface of the water! "An amphibious car!" marvels the Sage. "Sir Humphrey's more resourceful than I'd thought! We'll have to try to shake him off our trail!"

RUPERT REACHES UM ISLAND

"We'll have to hope Sir Humphrey's car
Finds travelling to Um too far . . ."

The Brella flies on through the night
And reaches Um as it grows light.

The Brella lands. "With luck we'll find
We've left Sir Humphrey's car behind!"

But then the goose points out to sea –
"Sir Humphrey!" gasps the Sage. "Dear me!"

"I'm afraid Sir Humphrey is trying to follow us!" says the Sage. "He knows we've got the golden goose and seems determined to catch it." "What if he reaches Um Island?" blinks Rupert. "The moment he sees the unicorns he'll try to capture them as well!" "You're right!" says the Sage. "We'll just have to hope he doesn't get that far . . ." The Brella speeds on across the sea until the sky lightens and dawn begins to break. "Land ahoy!" calls Rupert. "It's Um Island!"

As soon as they reach Um the Brella swoops down to land on a grassy slope above the rocky shore. "So far so good!" says the Sage. "I only hope Sir Humphrey has given up the chase and turned back towards the mainland . . ." Just then, the golden goose squawks in alarm and points out to sea, towards a dark shape approaching on the horizon. "Sir Humphrey!" gasps Rupert. "He hasn't given up at all! He must have been following us all through the night . . ."

RUPERT PLANS A SURPRISE

The Sage sets off across the isle
But Rupert stops and starts to smile . . .

"The unicorns! Together we
Can stop Sir Humphrey yet – you'll see . . ."

The friends all hide away before
Sir Humphrey's car reaches the shore . . .

"Look!" Scrogg calls out excitedly.
"The goose! Sir Humphrey! Follow me . . ."

The Sage decides that the best place to hide the goose is in a cave near the middle of the island. "Follow me!" he says. "We need to get there before the others arrive." As they set off Rupert hears an excited whinny and spots a unicorn galloping towards them, together with a little foal. "Hello!" cries the Sage. "I've brought some visitors with me. This is Rupert Bear, from Nutwood." Rupert strokes the foal and suddenly thinks of a way to trick Sir Humphrey . . .

By the time Sir Humphrey reaches the island, Rupert and the others have hidden themselves away, just near the spot where they first landed. "Good!" says Rupert as the car drives on to the sand. "They've come ashore at exactly the right place." "Um Island!" laughs Sir Humphrey. "Those fools have led us straight to it. All we have to do now is track down that dratted goose." "It's there!" calls Scrogg excitedly, pointing along the beach. "Quick, Boss! Come and help me catch it!"

RUPERT HIDES FROM VIEW

The goose spots Scrogg and runs away.
Sir Humphrey tries to make it stay . . .

Then suddenly they spot a sight
That fills Sir Humphrey with delight.

"The foal, Scrogg! Look, it's got a horn!
At last, I've found a unicorn!"

Another unicorn appears.
"She's the foal's mother!" Pumphrey cheers.

As soon as it spots Scrogg the goose runs off, away from the beach towards the middle of the island. "Come back!" calls Sir Humphrey. "There's no need for alarm. Scrogg and I can offer you a home. A haven for rare creatures! Trust me I . . ." All of a sudden, he stops in his tracks and stares ahead in wonder. "A unicorn!" gasps Scrogg. "I don't believe it!" whispers Sir Humphrey. "Careful, Scrogg! We don't want to frighten it off . . ."

Sir Humphrey stares at the baby unicorn in wonder. "All my life I've dreamt of finding one!" he murmurs. "It's amazing! Simply amazing!" "What about the goose?" asks Scrogg. "Leave it!" snaps his companion. "This is the prize we want! Imagine owning the only unicorn in captivity . . ." As he speaks, the foal turns to a grassy clearing where a full-grown unicorn appears. "Another one!" gasps Scrogg. "She must be the mother!" blinks Sir Humphrey. "How delightful!"

RUPERT FOOLS SIR HUMPHREY

"More unicorns!" Sir Humphrey cries.
"We've found a herd Scrogg! What a prize!"

"These unicorns are wild and free!
Not yours!" calls Rupert angrily.

"Sir Humphrey has a private zoo!
He plans to try to capture you . . ."

"Run, boss!" calls Scrogg. "Those unicorns
Are dangerous. Look at their horns!"

To the zoo-owner's delight, more unicorns join the foal and its mother in the grassy clearing. "There's a whole herd!" he calls to Scrogg. "The last unicorns in the world, and they're ours for the taking . . ." "No they're not!" cries Rupert, suddenly emerging from his hiding place. "The unicorns are wild creatures which live here in peace. Nobody owns them, and nobody ever will!" "That's what you think!" glowers Sir Humphrey. "This time, nothing will stand in my way!"

To Sir Humphrey's surprise, Rupert is joined by more and more unicorns, who lower their horns menacingly. "They don't look very friendly!" gasps Scrogg. "These men threaten your island!" calls Rupert. "They tried to catch the golden goose and now they want to catch you too!" "Look out, boss!" calls Scrogg. "Run for your life!" The goose honks loudly and the unicorns begin to charge. "Back to the car!" cries Sir Humphrey. "Hurrah!" laughs Rupert. "Our plan's working . . ."

RUPERT SAVES THE GOLDEN GOOSE

The men keep running till they reach
The car they've left parked on the beach . . .

"Bravo!" laughs Rupert. "That was fun!
Sir Humphrey's given up! We've won!"

"Good!" laughs the Sage. "I don't think they
Will trouble us again today."

"I know the very place for you!
Where lots of other birds live too . . ."

Pursued by the unicorns, Sir Humphrey and Scrogg scramble down to the beach and race back towards their car. "They're getting closer!" wails Scrogg. "I can hear the thunder of hooves . . ." "Keep running!" puffs his chief. "There isn't much further to go!" The two men leap into the car and drive off without a backward glance. "Good riddance!" cheers Rupert as he watches them put to sea. The goose honks and the unicorns all neigh delightedly.

"Well done!" cries the Sage. "You gave Sir Humphrey and Scrogg such a fright they forgot all about our feathered friend . . ." The goose picks up Scrogg's cap and carries it off as a trophy. "Do you think they'll ever come back?" asks Rupert. "They might!" says the Sage, "Although I don't think they'll try to catch any more unicorns!" Turning to the goose, he declares that he's thought of an even better home for it than Um Island. "It's just the place for a special bird!"

RUPERT MEETS THE BIRD KING

The Brella flies across the sea –
Where can its destination be?

"A castle!" Rupert gives a cry –
"The Bird King's Palace in the sky!"

The Brella lands. A guard asks who
They are and what they've come to do . . .

"We've brought a bird for you to see.
It's very rare, Your Majesty!"

Rupert is mystified. "Where can be safer than Um Island?" he thinks. "Climb aboard the Brella and you'll soon find out!" smiles the Sage. "I'll take you there straightaway." The unicorns gather to bid farewell to Rupert as the Brella speeds out to sea. Climbing higher and higher, it emerges above the clouds in a haze of dazzling sunshine . . . Ahead of them, Rupert spots the turrets of a large castle. "The Bird King's Palace!" he cries. "I should have guessed! It's the perfect hideaway!"

As the Brella lands, an astonished guard comes hurrying to meet it. "Hello!" calls Rupert. "We've come from Um Island, with a special visitor to see your King . . ." The Bird King is told of Rupert's arrival and agrees to see him immediately. "A special visitor, Your Majesty!" declares the guard. "The Sage of Um?" asks the King. "No!" laughs Rupert. "The Sage and I have brought you a special bird to join your flock." "A bird!" blinks the King. "Let us see it straightaway!"

RUPERT SAYS GOODBYE

"A golden egg!" the Bird King cries,
Unable to believe his eyes . . .

The King says the gold eggs can be
Stored safely in his Treasury.

"I'll tell the other geese where you
Are living – they can visit too . . ."

"Just wait till Odmedod hears how
The goose has found a safe home now!"

The goose steps forward with a gleaming golden egg. "Can this be true?" gasps the King. "I have heard tell of such things in my grandfather's time, but I never dreamt of a golden goose gracing Our Court!" The King is so pleased that he puts the goose in charge of the Royal Treasury. "Your golden eggs will be stored in our strongroom, safe from all treasure-seekers!" he declares. "From now on, you will dwell among friends and enjoy the protection of the entire Palace Guard!"

Rupert and the Sage are delighted that the goose has found a proper home. "I'll tell Farmer Brown's geese where you are!" Rupert promises. The golden goose beams delightedly as the King thanks the pair for all they've done. "I'll take you back to Nutwood now!" smiles the Sage as he and Rupert leave in the Brella. "Thanks!" says Rupert. "Just wait till Odmedod hears everything that's happened!"

Make Your Own Butterfly Cakes

Ask an adult to help

Follow this recipe carefully and you can make your very own batch of butterfly cakes. They may not fly, but they should taste delicious.

INGREDIENTS:

(makes 12 cakes)

110g butter
110g caster sugar
2 eggs
110g self-raising flour
A pinch of salt
1 tsp vanilla essence
1 quantity of buttercream *(for the topping, see below)*
Icing sugar

INSTRUCTIONS:

1. Pre-heat an oven to 190°c (Gas mark 5)

2. Grease a bun tray with butter or line with individual paper cases.

3. Beat the butter in a bowl with a wooden spoon until it is soft. Add the caster sugar and vanilla essence and keep stirring until the mixture is light and fluffy.

4. Crack the eggs into a separate bowl and beat thoroughly.

5. Add beaten eggs to the mixture a little at a time, use a metal spoon to gradually fold in the sifted flour and salt. Beat until final mixture is soft and creamy.

6. Use a spoon to half-fill each mould or paper case.

7. Bake in the pre-heated oven for 15-20 minutes, until cakes are golden and well-risen. Allow cakes to cool on a wire rack.

TO MAKE BUTTERCREAM

INGREDIENTS:

50g butter
100g icing sugar
2-3 drops vanilla essence
1-2 tbsp milk

1. Beat softened butter until creamy.

2. Gradually add sifted icing sugar and a few drops of vanilla essence.

3. Add enough milk to ensure a creamy texture. (You can use 2 tbsp of freshly squeezed orange juice instead of the vanilla essence and milk if you prefer a different flavour Icing.)

---

8. When the cakes have cooled, slice off the top of each one and spoon on a little buttercream.

9. Cut the original top of each cake in half and stand these in the buttercream like the wings of a butterfly.

10. Lightly dust the cakes with icing sugar. Now eat them before they fly away . . .

RUPERT®

and the

Magical Cabinet

RUPERT MEETS THE MAGIC MAN

At breakfast, Rupert's full of cheer.
His summertime is nearly here!

But what's that noise? He spies a van,
And then out steps a well-dressed man.

"I'm due at Nutwood School today,
If you could kindly point the way?"

The bear replies, "I'll show you how:
Just follow us! We'll head there now."

It was a glorious summer morning and Rupert was in good spirits. "Well now," his Mummy exclaims, "you do look cheerful. Are you nearly ready for your holidays?" "Oh yes," the little bear smiles. He likes his school and his teacher Dr Chimp, but he can't help but feel excited that it is the last day of term. "By this time tomorrow, I shall be at the seaside!" he thinks. Rupert is about to leave for school when he spies a large van approaching. "I wonder who that could be?"

Out steps a well-dressed man. "Excuse me," he begins. "I'm afraid I'm rather lost. You see, I'm a stage magician, and I've been booked to entertain the pupils at Nutwood School for their last day of term." Rupert sees the words 'Mr Magic Man' painted on the side of his van. "I'm wonderful at magic but terrible at directions," the man chuckles. "I don't suppose you could tell me the way?" "I can help!" Rupert offers. "Just follow me there . . ."

RUPERT LENDS A HAND

As they arrive, the bear explains:
"Just one more day of term remains!"

"That's why I'm here," the man replies.
"I'm doing magic tricks. Surprise!"

"We'll help unload. It won't take long!"
Says Rupert, feeling rather strong.

They help the man arrange his set.
"But wait!" he calls. "We're not done yet."

Rupert runs along the path, with the Magic Man driving slowly behind him. The little bear waves to his chums along the way. Soon they all arrive at Nutwood School, where Dr Chimp is there to greet them. "Thank you kindly, Rupert Bear," the Magic Man says, stepping out of his van. Inside, Rupert sees someone sitting in the passenger's seat . . . "Wait a minute!" Rupert exclaims. "That must be a ventriloquist dummy!" The Magic Man laughs. "This is Madera, my assistant!" he replies.

The van is filled with an assortment of boxes of all sizes – the Magic Man's tricks for his performance today. Rupert and his chums offer to help carry the boxes inside. "I'll take the heavy one," Edward Trunk says. Bill Badger and Algy Pug lift the medium-sized boxes, with Podgy Pig carrying a chair. They set them down on the stage, so the Magic Man can start unpacking. He mutters, "there's just one more thing to bring in, but I'll need everyone's help . . ."

RUPERT CARRIES THE CABINET

There's one more trick to bring inside:
A cabinet that's tall and wide.

"I haven't tried this trick before,"
He says, but won't tell any more . . .

The pupils start to clap and shout,
Then: "Hush, now!" Dr Chimp calls out.

"May I present Madera, too?"
The dummy adds, "How do you do?"

It takes four of the chums to lift the final piece of equipment. It appears to be an ornately decorated cabinet that is even taller than Dr Chimp, and Rupert wonders what's stored inside. When he asks, the Magic Man explains that the cabinet is his newest trick. "Well, what magic does it do?" Rupert questions. "Yes, do tell us!" his chums beg. The Magic Man just winks. "You'll soon find out. But I'm very excited, because it will be my first time performing this trick!"

The morning passes quickly, and soon it's time for the magic show! Dr Chimp leads all the pupils into the hall. "Settle down," he says kindly. But his words are soon forgotten as the Magic Man steps forwards on the stage, and the audience burst into thunderous applause. "Greetings, one and all!" he booms. "May I introduce myself – the Magic Man – and my assistant here – Madera!" "Oh yes, Madera, that's me!" the ventriloquist dummy mouths. "How do you do?"

RUPERT ENJOYS THE MAGIC TRICKS

They act out tricks for everyone.
Cheers Gregory: "An egg? How fun!"

Bunting's pulled from Edward's vest.
The elephant is most impressed!

Next, Podgy Pig can't help but grin,
When blooms appear beneath his chin.

He deftly conjures – from thin air –
A shining coin for Rupert Bear.

"Madera is a most brilliant assistant," the Magic Man continues. "Yes, very brilliant!" Madera echoes, and the pupils laugh. "Do you want to see what Madera can do?" asks the Magic Man. "Yes!" everyone cheers. First, Madera "pulls" an egg from behind Gregory's ear. "Oh goodness," squeaks the little Guinea-Pig. "I didn't know that was there!" Rupert can see the Magic Man moving his dummy's arm, but he is still amazed at the tricks they perform together.

Madera reaches into Edward's vest, and reveals a long length of colourful bunting. Edward gasps. "How did you do that?" But neither the Magic Man or Madera give the secret away! Next, they approach Podgy Pig and reach into his pocket. "There's nothing in there but an extra sandwich," Podgy begins, yet out comes – not a sandwich, but a large bouquet of flowers! Finally, it's Rupert Bear's turn. Madera plucks a shiny gold coin from underneath his scarf. The bear is awestruck.

RUPERT ENJOYS THE ORIGAMI

He sits Madera on a chair,
Then chuckles: "But let's not stop there!"

With skilful folds, he holds up high,
A charming paper butterfly.

"It's origami!" Rupert thinks,
"But what's the trick?" The old man winks.

With one great whoosh, the papers zoom,
As butterflies flap 'round the room!

"That's a lot of magic tricks," Madera tells the crowd, "I'm getting a bit tired!" "Now Madera, would you like to have a rest?" the Magic Man replies. "You just sit down in this chair here, and then I'll perform some magic." He pulls a sheet of brightly coloured paper from his waistcoat pocket, and folds it carefully: first down the middle, and then in half again. Rupert recognises that he's making an origami butterfly. "But I wonder what trick he'll do?" he whispers to Bill Badger.

Before Bill can answer, the Magic Man cups the paper butterfly in his palms. He blows softly into his hands and then asks Rupert to blow as well. "And just like magic . . ." the man whispers, opening up his hands . . . Rupert and the others all gasp, as the single paper butterfly has become a whole flock of colourful origami butterflies, fluttering around the stage. They whoosh through the air . . . and one lands briefly on Rupert Bear's ear! "That tickles!" he laughs.

RUPERT WATCHES MADERA DISAPPEAR

The magic show has gone too fast –
This coming trick will be his last.

"I'll close the magic box up here,
To make Madera disappear!"

He gives his magic wand a flick.
Soon stars appear – it's quite the trick!

He pulls the door, to show inside:
The chair is now unoccupied!

Rupert and his chums would gladly watch the Magic Man all day, but the show is coming to a close. "I have one final trick for you," he proclaims, and Rupert Bear can hardly hide his disappointment that the fun is nearly over. "At least we'll get to find out about the mysterious cabinet!" he thinks. On stage, the Magic Man taps all four sides of the cabinet, and unlocks the door with a tiny, golden key. "Madera, are you ready?"

"I'm ready!" Madera responds. "Are you sure?" the Magic Man teases. "This is a brand-new trick, so it's not without risk." But Madera gives a smile as the Magic Man puts the him inside the cabinet, closes the door and then waves his magic wand. The stage is filled with sparkles, stars and a puff of smoke. After whispering his magic words, the Magic Man opens the cabinet door to reveal . . . an empty chair! "He made Madera disappear! Bravo! What a trick!" the pupils cry out.

RUPERT EXAMINES THE CABINET

"Let's bring him back!" He shuts the door,
And waves his magic wand once more.

It doesn't take him very long,
To recognise the trick's gone wrong!

Then Dr Chimp says, "Come with me.
I think we need a cup of tea."

The chums explore the magic box.
But – who's that? Is it Freddy Fox?

It's a wonderful finale, but it's time to bring Madera back. The Magic Man closes the door again, and taps the sides of the cabinet one by one. He flourishes his wand once more, summoning more smoke and stars. He reaches for the handle and opens the door dramatically. "Now Madera is ba–" But the Magic Man never finishes what he was going to say, because the chair in the cabinet is still empty. Something has gone terribly wrong with his trick!

Dr Chimp runs up onto the stage to console the Magic Man. "But . . . Madera . . . was supposed to . . . come back!" the Magic Man gasps. "Why don't you come to my office for a cup of tea," Dr Chimp says soothingly. Rupert and his chums are left in the hall, examining the cabinet. "We all carried it in earlier, so what could have happened?" Rupert mutters. He's so lost in thought that he doesn't notice Freddy and Ferdy Fox behind him.

There's nothing to be done before
Those naughty Foxes slam the door.

With Bill and Rupert trapped inside,
The Foxes run away to hide.

Then Podgy shouts: "They've vanished, too!
If only we knew what to do . . ."

But as for Bill and Rupert Bear –
They're swiftly whizzing through the air . . .

The naughty Fox brothers are bored now that the magic show is over, and looking to pull off a trick of their own! Freddy pushes the cabinet door closed with Rupert and Bill still inside. "Say 'please' and we'll let you out," Freddy teases. But Ferdy has been twirling the Magic Man's wand playfully . . . and the smoke and stars reappear! There's a shout from inside the cabinet, but then silence! The foxes panic and run off, dropping the wand behind them . . .

Edward Trunk opens the door to let his chums out. "They're both gone!" he exclaims. "We'd better go and tell Dr Chimp right away," Algy Pug suggests. Podgy just points frantically at the empty chair. Meanwhile, Rupert and Bill are whizzing through the air. Rupert blinks, and he sees cards, magic wands, a white dove . . . and is that a rabbit in a top hat? Everything is moving so quickly . . . and a moment later, they land on the ground with a soft bump.

RUPERT ARRIVES IN MAGIC LAND

And soon they land, then gaze around,
At all the treasures on the ground.

The bear is stunned. "Just look at that:
A rabbit bouncing in a hat!"

"Do come with me," the rabbit pleads,
And so they follow where it leads.

They reach a quiet home, and then,
A carpenter invites them in.

Rupert sits up and rubs his eyes. "Where do you think we are?" Bill asks him. Rupert doesn't know, but he's very glad that his chum is there with him! All around, he can see traces of magical items, and a soft breeze ripples through giant flowers. Though strange, it is a very pleasant place to be. Just then, something bounces up beside him. "It's a rabbit . . . bouncing in a top hat!" Rupert remarks. Now he's sure this was the rabbit he saw earlier!

"You must follow me at once!" the rabbit says. "Just when I thought things couldn't get stranger, the rabbit is talking to us . . ." Bill mutters. "Please," the rabbit continues, and the chums decide it is their best course of action. The rabbit leads the way, bouncing along in the hat. They haven't gone far when they arrive at a small cottage. The rabbit whistles, and a little man, his workbelt overflowing with strange looking tools, emerges from the cottage.

The old man's dummy waves his hand,
He's come to life in Magic Land!

They all sit down to drink their tea,
While Rupert tells what came to be.

"A magic cabinet, you say?
I'll help you both home, straight away!"

The kindly builder looks about.
"Madera, would you help me out?"

"Well, well . . . welcome to the Land of Enchantment!" the little man trills. "Do come inside my workshop." "Yes, come inside!" calls a voice that sounds oddly familiar . . . when Rupert and Bill step inside, they are astonished to see Madera sitting at the table. Only this time it's not the Magic Man moving him and speaking for him. Somehow, Madera has fully come to life! "I think you both need a cup of tea and some nice cakes . . ."

Rupert and Bill take turns to explain what happened. "You arrived through the cabinet, too eh?" says the man. "I know all about cabinets – I'm a Master Magic Cabinet Maker, you see. Your magic man needed a cabinet that only gave the illusion of making someone disappear. But it must have gotten mixed up with one of my magical cabinets!" "Can you send us home then?" Rupert asks. "Yes, but I'll need Madera's help . . ."

"This cloud will take you home, I hope.
Just climb up on this little rope."

But though the chums climb way up high,
The cloud is stuck, and cannot fly.

"We'll get you home soon. Have no fear . . .
Let's try my teleporter here . . ."

Yet once again, it goes awry.
"We're trapped," thinks Rupert, with a sigh.

The Cabinet Maker explains that he can't send them back the way they came, but he has another plan! "The old rope trick should do it!" Madera helps him bring a large basket into the middle of the room. With a wave of his hands, a small cloud appears above the basket. "Grab the rope as it comes out," he calls to the chums, "and the magic cloud will carry you home." Soon, Rupert and Bill reach the cloud, but . . . nothing happens. "We're stuck!" Bill calls.

"Oh dear! Not to worry – as a Master Magician, I have many things up my sleeve!" The little man shows Rupert and Bill his glowing Teleporter machine. "Where did you say you came from?" he asks, fiddling with the dials. "Nutwood, please," Rupert replies. "That should do it," the little man says. "Just hop right in . . ." There is a loud 'POP!', and Rupert and Bill have vanished. But not to Nutwood . . . they've only made it as far as the top of the cabinet on the other side of the room!

RUPERT FLIES WITH A DRAGON

"A dragon? Yes! That's what we'll do!
I'll conjure one up now for you!"

At last, the magic spell goes right,
The dragon grows, and soon takes flight.

They're home before too long. "Hooray!"
Calls Rupert. "It's been quite the day!"

The dragon fades, but all around,
Snapdragons grow across the ground.

The Cabinet Maker is a little flustered, but he has one more idea. "Hmmm, I wonder . . ." He pulls a handkerchief from his pocket and snaps his fingers. Suddenly, there is a small, pink dragon wriggling in his palm. Rupert gasps. His eyes grow wide as the dragon begins to grow . . . and grow . . . and grow . . . until he is the size of a large horse. "This is a magical Snap Dragon," he tells Rupert and Bill. "Just whisper where you want to go, and he will fly you there."

Rupert and Bill hold tight to the dragon and wave goodbye to the little man and to Madera, who has decided to stay behind in the Land of Enchantment. The Snap Dragon soars into the sky . . . and before they know it, they're back at school. Their chums Cabinet amazed at the sight of their pals arriving home and they listen as Bill tells them of their adventures. Meanwhile, Rupert watches as the magical Snap Dragon quietly fades away into a beautiful carpet of pink flowers.

RUPERT GOES ON HIS HOLIDAY

That night, the bear has much to tell –
Though strange, his day has ended well!

The next day – to the Bears' surprise –
They see a face they recognise!

"I'm just so glad that you're all right.
Please come to see my show tonight?"

The Bears decide they want to go,
And see the old man's magic show.

That evening, while packing for their summer holiday, Rupert tells his parents about his adventure with the Magic Man and Madera. "It sounds like a very unusual last day of term," Mr Bear chuckles. The very next day, the Bears get up early to drive to the seaside. Who should they see there, but . . ."It's the Magic Man again!" Rupert shouts, and he calls out to his friend. The Magic Man is surprised and delighted to see him.

"I'm so sorry about the mix-up with the cabinet," he says. "I visited the Cabinet Maker and everything should be fixed now. I was so pleased to see my dear friend Madera is happily employed as his assistant in the Land of Enchantment too." The Magic Man invites all three Bears to the theatre later that day to see his show, and Rupert's parents are most intrigued. "It will be a great show . . ." Rupert thinks.

RUPERT TRIES THE TRICK AGAIN

He needs someone to volunteer . . .
"Yes, Rupert! You can disappear."

"And now you see him . . . now he's gone . . ."
The trick is fixed! He carries on!

As Rupert Bear peeks out the door,
The rabbit tumbles to the floor!

There's loud applause from everyone –
They know this summer will be fun!

Once again, the audience is captivated by the Magic Man's performance. "And for my next trick, I need a volunteer . . ." he calls. Before he knows what he's doing, Rupert has put his hand up, and the Magic Man brings him to the stage. "Shall we make you 'disappear' again?" the Magic Man says with a wink, as Rupert steps into the magical cabinet. The magician flourishes his wand, says the magic words and checks inside the cabinet. Rupert has disappeared!

He waves his wand again and opens the cabinet door once more . . . and Rupert steps out! The crowd applauds enthusiastically. But then, something else pops out of the cabinet . . . it's the rabbit in the top hat! "Oh dear, a stowaway?" Rupert chuckles. The rabbit bounces off before anyone can stop him. As he watches the Magic Man chase after the rabbit, Rupert thinks to himself, it's going to be a very magical summer!

Spot the Difference

It's been a magical day and Rupert and his pals have had lots of fun.
There are ten differences between the two pictures. Can you spot them all?

Answers: 1) The lilac butterfly has disappeared, 2) Bill has been replaced with Gertie the goose, 3) the house has changed to a castle turret, 4) the bunny in the top hat has changed to a duck, 5) the Magician is now holding Madeira, 6) Edward is now wearing his cap, 7) Edward's scarf has changed colour, 8) the windows have changed, 9) the bunting has changed colour, 10) Gregory has disappeared and Bill is in his place.

HOW TO MAKE A BUTTERFLY

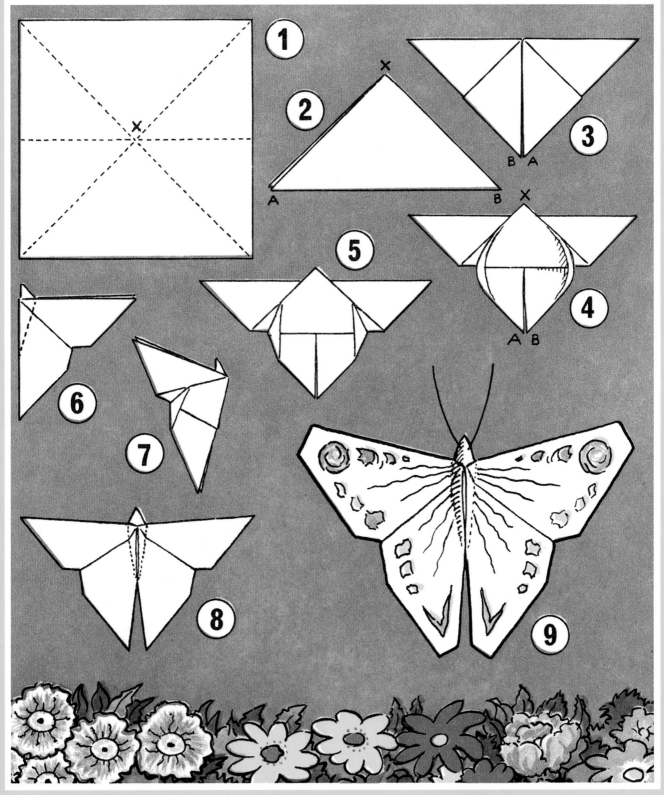

Did you spot the Magic Man making origami butterflies in Rupert and the Magical Cabinet? To make your own, take a square of thin paper, fold opposite corners together both ways, turn the paper over and fold side to side one way, so that the creases are as in Figure 1. Pinch all corners and drop in the sides (Fig. 2). Lift A and B to X, press firmly and turn the paper the other way up (Fig. 3). Now turn the paper over and lift X up rather higher than the top edge (Fig. 4) and press the new folds (Fig. 5). Fold the model in half (Fig. 6), mark a dotted line on each side, and bring both wings forward, pressing firmly along both dotted lines (Fig. 7). Open out and there is your butterfly (Fig. 8). You can then fold inward the four points, paint the wings and stick two bristles on the head (Fig. 9). This pretty model is a favourite of the expert paper-folder Akira Yoshizawa of Tokyo.

RUPERT and

It's nearly Christmas – time to go
Out carol singing in the snow . . .

It is nearly Christmas and Rupert is going carol singing with some of his friends. "Wrap up warm, dear," says his mother. "It's snowing outside!" "Deep and crisp and even!" chuckles Mr Bear. "Just like the carol!" A few moments later, the doorbell rings, "It's Ottoline!" cries Rupert. "Hello!" she smiles. "I see you've got a lantern too. We'd better set off immediately, so we don't keep Dr Chimp and the others waiting . . ."

Santa's Present

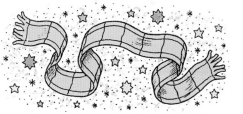

"Hello" says Ottoline. "I see
You've got a lantern – just like me!"

"More snow!" says Ottoline. "What fun!
We'll light the way for everyone!"

"I love the snow!" laughs Ottoline as the two pals hurry along. "Me too!" says Rupert. "If it keeps falling, there should be enough to build snowmen tomorrow." By the time the pair arrive, Dr Chimp and the others are all ready to start. "Hello!" he calls. "I've made a list of the carols we're going to sing, starting with Silent Night. Algy Pug's brought his trumpet along, so if you forget the tune just listen to him."

"Hello!" says Dr Chimp. "You're all
Here now – so let's make our first call . . ."

RUPERT GOES CAROL SINGING

"Well done!" Mr Anteater cheers.
"The best singing I've heard for years!"

When Mrs Sheep hears them begin,
She's so delighted she joins in!

"This way now everybody, our
Last call's the old Professor's tower!"

The pals start. Rupert rings the bell,
Then sings King Wenceslas as well . . .

Everyone in Nutwood looks forward to the carol singers and comes hurrying out to greet them as soon as they appear. "Well done!" chuckles Mr Anteater. "Reminds me of when I was a youngster. Before your time, Dr Chimp, but we sang carols even then, you know!" "Lovely!" smiles Mrs Sheep, joining in the last verse. "Can I ask you all in for a mince pie and tea?" "That's very kind," says Dr Chimp, "but we can't stop yet. There are a few more houses left to visit . . ."

At last, the carol singers have visited almost everyone in Nutwood. "Just one more call before we go home," declares Dr Chimp and leads the way across the snow to the old Professor's tower . . . "Good King Wenceslas!" he whispers. "Sing up, everyone. As loud as you can!" "Happy Christmas!" calls Rupert, tugging the bell-pull as the others begin. "The Professor's bound to ask us in," he thinks. "Last year we had tea in his study, while Bodkin cut a special cake."

RUPERT IS PUZZLED

The music ends, but no-one comes
To greet the disappointed chums!

"How strange!" thinks Rupert. "Not a light
Is burning in the tower tonight . . ."

Next morning, he goes back to see
If he can solve the mystery.

He rings the bell but the front door
Stays shut, just as it did before . . .

To Rupert's surprise, the carol ends and nobody comes to the door . . . "Perhaps he didn't hear us?" says Gregory. "Impossible!" says Algy. "He must have gone away for Christmas." "What a pity!" says Dr Chimp. "Oh well, we'd better be getting home. Thank you all for singing so well, and thank you, Algy, for playing the trumpet!" "I wonder if the Professor has really gone away?" thinks Rupert. He glances back towards the tower but all the windows are dark and nobody stirs.

Next morning, Rupert decides to go back to the Professor's tower to see if there is any sign of his old friend. In the daylight everything looks much more welcoming, with the Professor's flag fluttering in the breeze to let everyone know he's there. When he reaches the tower, Rupert pulls the bell as hard as he can. He hears it ring inside, but nobody comes to the door. "I wonder what's wrong?" he thinks. "I'd better try again, to make sure they know I'm here . . ."

RUPERT FINDS A STRANGE MIRROR

He tries the door. To his surprise
It isn't locked. "Hello!" he cries.

"Where can the old Professor be?
I'll look in the laboratory . . ."

"A mirror – with a strange machine!
It isn't one I've ever seen . . ."

"Astonishing! My hand can pass
Straight through this sheet of solid glass!"

As he waits for a reply, Rupert pushes at the door, only to find that it swings open straightaway. "Hello!" he calls. "Is anybody there?" No one replies as Rupert steps inside. "The Professor's probably hard at work," he thinks. "The door must open automatically." Making his way to the Professor's laboratory, he spots a strange new machine, set in front of a large mirror. "It's still switched on," he blinks. "The Professor can't have gone very far . . ."

Fascinated by the Professor's laboratory, Rupert can't resist taking a closer look at his latest invention. "How odd!" he gasps. "It looks like a mirror, but I can't see my reflection!" The longer he peers at it, the stranger it seems. "It's like a giant window," Rupert murmurs and reaches out to tap the glass. To his astonishment, his hand passes straight through without meeting any resistance. "Goodness!" he gasps. "It isn't a window either!"

RUPERT STEPS THROUGH THE MIRROR

He steps right through the glass but then
Emerges in the lab again!

"It felt just like an empty frame,
But nothing this side looks the same!"

Then Bodkin suddenly appears.
"I've found you at last!" Rupert cheers.

"No visitors! My master's too
Important to see scamps like you!"

Stepping forward, Rupert passes straight through the mirror and finds himself back in the laboratory, exactly where he started . . . "Just like an empty frame!" he thinks, then suddenly notices that everything looks strange. "That's not the Professor's machine!" he gasps. "It's smaller and a different shape. Nothing's the same!" he thinks. "I wonder where I am?" Just then he hears voices outside and somebody walking towards the door. "Who's there?" a voice calls angrily . . .

"Bodkin!" cries Rupert. "Thank goodness it's you. I was beginning to think . . ." "What are you doing here?" snaps the little servant. "The Professor doesn't allow strangers in his laboratory. He's hard at work and left strict instructions not to be disturbed . . ." "Strangers?" gasps Rupert. "But we're friends . . ." "Friends?" scoffs the servant. "Why should the Professor be friends with an urchin like you? Be off this instant, before I call a policeman and report you for trespassing!"

RUPERT SPOTS HIS PALS

"There's something else wrong!" Rupert thinks.
"The snow's all disappeared!" he blinks.

Then Rupert hears a distant call
And spots his chums, all playing ball.

He runs towards them, glad to see
That they're still acting normally . . .

But, as he joins them, they all say
They thought he'd gone on holiday!

Astonished by Bodkin's outburst, Rupert is even more surprised as he turns to leave the Professor's tower. "The snow!" he gasps. "It's disappeared . . ." Everywhere Rupert looks, brightly-coloured flowers are in full bloom, while the sun shines down as if it were a summer's day. "W . . . what's happened?" he asks, then catches sight of a group of chums, playing football on the Common. "I wonder if they've noticed how hot it's suddenly become?"

When Rupert joins his pals, they all seem startled to see him. "Hello Trepur, what are you doing here?" cries Algy. "I thought you'd gone on holiday!" "No," says Rupert. "We never go away at Christmas . . ." "I thought you'd gone too!" shrugs Willie Mouse. "Never mind. Why don't you come and join the game?" "Thanks!" says Rupert. "But there's something I wanted to ask you . . ." "What's that?" says Bill. "I . . . I say!" gasps Rupert. "You're all wearing different clothes."

RUPERT SEES SANTA'S SLEIGH

When Rupert tells them where he's been
They say its Nikdob he's just seen . . .

"Forget about him! Join the fun.
He's always cross with everyone!"

The game ends. All the pals have brought
A Christmas present of some sort . . .

For Santa Claus!" says Bill. "We leave
Him presents every Christmas Eve!"

"Different clothes?" laughs Willie. "But this is what I always wear! What did you want to know?" "The . . . the Professor," stammers Rupert. "I went to see him, but Bodkin wouldn't let me in!" "Nikdob, you mean," cry the pals. "You should have known better to ask him! He's always so cross . . . The Professor's just as grumpy. He claims that visitors interrupt his work!" "Come on!" cries Willie, kicking the ball. Rupert joins in but still feels puzzled. Why is everything so strange?

As soon as the game is over, the pals tell Rupert they've got some Christmas presents for Santa . . . "What a good idea!" he cries. "I don't expect anyone has ever given him a present before." "But that's what we do every year!" blinks Algy. "Come on!" calls Bill. "Let's go to look for the sleigh. It should be waiting by the edge of the Common . . ." Sure enough, Rupert soon spots Santa's sleigh, with one of his helpers loading presents into a sack . . .

RUPERT RIDES IN THE SLEIGH

"Thanks!" Santa's helper smiles as they
All load their gifts aboard the sleigh.

"I've brought Santa a present too . . .
Please can I take it back with you?"

"Yes," says the helper. "In you hop!
We're off now. This is our last stop."

"I'll ask Santa and see if he
Knows where the Professor can be . . . "

"Thank you!" says the little man as he accepts the chums' gifts. "It was very kind of you to write and ask Santa what he wanted this year . . ." "How odd!" thinks Rupert. "Everything seems to be back to front!" "Have you brought anything?" asks Algy. "No," begins Rupert, then he suddenly has an idea. "Santa must get jolly cold at the North Pole," he tells the helper. "I'd like to give him a warm scarf. Can I come with you and deliver it myself?"

The little helper thinks hard for a moment, then gives a broad smile. "Of course you can come," he tells Rupert. "Hop aboard and I'll take you with me!" As soon as Rupert is ready, the reindeer bound forward and Santa's sleigh takes off. "Goodbye!" call the chums, all waving excitedly. As the sleigh rises high above Nutwood, Rupert spots the old Professor's tower. "That's where the mystery began," he murmurs. "Perhaps Santa will be able to tell me what's happened . . ."

RUPERT VISITS SANTA'S CASTLE

"There's Santa's castle, drawing near,
But what if he's changed too? Oh, dear!"

The sleigh arrives. "Can Rupert please
See Santa?" "Yes," a guard agrees.

As soon as Santa sees who's there
He smiles. "Bless me! It's Rupert Bear!"

"But you're from Nutwood! Tell me how
You managed to arrive just now . . ."

On and on speeds Santa's sleigh, over forests and mountains, until Nutwood has been left far behind. The little helper calls to the reindeer which soar even higher, up through the clouds. "There's Santa's castle!" cries Rupert. "I hope it hasn't changed too . . ." Landing in the castle courtyard, the helper leads Rupert to the main gate. "A visitor for Santa!" he tells one of the guards. "Please can I see him?" asks Rupert. "I know he's very busy, but there's something I need to ask . . ."

"Follow me!" calls the sentry and leads Rupert up a flight of steps to Santa's study. "Visitor, sir!" he calls. "Visitor?" asks Santa. "Why, it's Rupert Bear, from Nutwood . . ." "That's right!" smiles Rupert. "At least, I think it's Nutwood I came from. Everything there seems so different, I'm not really sure . . ." "How did you get here?" asks Santa. "On the sleigh, with all your presents," explains Rupert. "My presents?" gasps Santa. "But they're not from Nutwood at all!"

RUPERT ASKS FOR HELP

"Ah!" Santa cries. "I understand!
You've travelled here from Mirror Land!"

"It's Nutwood – but the wrong way round!
Hence all the changes that you found . . ."

"From what you say, it seems to me
That's where the Professor must be!"

The pair fly off in Santa's sleigh
To Mirror Land, without delay . . .

"People in Nutwood don't send me presents!" explains Santa. "They're from Mirror Land . . ." "Mirror Land?" gasps Rupert. "The opposite to everything you know!" laughs Santa. "It looks like Nutwood but everything's different because it's on the wrong side of the mirror." "The Professor!" cries Rupert. "That must be why he's disappeared. His new machine took him to Mirror Land – and he hasn't come back!" "Goodness!" blinks Santa. "We'd better go and find him . . ."

As Santa leads the way to the courtyard, Rupert tells him all about the Professor's disappearance and how he found a strange mirror in the empty laboratory . . ." "A doorway to Mirror Land!" cries Santa. "Then that's where we'll find him!" Climbing aboard the sleigh, he calls to his reindeer, who gallop up into the sky. "Hold tight!" he warns Rupert as they soar over the castle ramparts. "I've told my reindeer to take us back to Mirror Land as quickly as they can."

RUPERT SPOTS A LIGHT

They reach the tower as darkness falls.
"A light's been switched on!" Rupert calls.

"That's Nikdob's master! Never fear!
No-one will see us land up here . . ."

"This way!" says Santa. "In we go!
We"ll search the tower from top to toe . . ."

"Stay close to me! Don't lag behind.
And not a sound of any kind!"

It is dark by the time Rupert and Santa reach their destination, with the stars twinkling in the sky and only the moon to light their way . . . "Look!" whispers Rupert as they near the tower, "There's a light on in the window!" "Somebody's still awake," says Santa. "But I don't suppose they're expecting any visitors . . ." Pulling gently on the reins, he lands silently on the roof. "Well done," he whispers to the reindeer. "Now we'll see if the Professor's still inside . . ."

Rupert follows Santa, but hesitates as he reaches the little door at the top of the tower. "What about Nikdob?" he asks. "He isn't very friendly . . ." "Of course not!" laughs Santa. "He's the exact opposite of the Professor's servant, Bodkin. One is pleasant and welcoming, while the other's bad-tempered and surly. Don't worry," he adds. "We can look for the Professor without Nikdob or his master ever knowing . . ." "How?" blinks Rupert, but Santa is already climbing down the winding steps.

RUPERT SEES NIKDOB'S MASTER

"There's Nikdob and his master now!
We'll have to both get past somehow . . ."

"My sleeping powder!" Santa cries.
"Stand still, Rupert – and shut your eyes!"

The magic dust swirls through the air
And bright stars shimmer everywhere . . .

"Good!" Santa smiles. "Those two won't wake
No matter how much noise we make!"

Rupert and Santa tiptoe along a gloomy corridor until they spot Nikdob and his master, sitting by the fire. "He's just like the Professor!" gasps Rupert. "Almost," nods Santa, but he'd be just as cross as Nikdob if he knew we were here." Reaching deep into his pocket, the old man brings out a small sack and tells Rupert to cover his eyes. "I'm going to make sure they don't disturb us!" he whispers. "If we're to find the Professor we need to be able to search the whole tower."

As Rupert shuts his eyes, Santa opens the sack and sprinkles a handful of powder into the room. "Sleepy-dust!" he declares. "It's what I use to make sure children are fast asleep when I come to deliver their presents." Sure enough, when Rupert peers into the room, Bodkin and his master are sound asleep, surrounded by shimmering stars. "If you hadn't closed your eyes, you'd be sleeping too!" chuckles Santa. Leaving the pair to snooze by the fire, he sets off to begin the search . . .

RUPERT FREES THE PROFESSOR

"Professor!" the pair start to call
But nobody replies at all . . .

Then Rupert spots some steps that go
Down to the basement, far below . . .

He clambers down and hears a shout –
"How dare you? Come and let us out!"

"The Professor!" he turns a key
And sets the missing couple free!

Rupert and Santa search the tower for signs of the old Professor. "Hello!" calls Santa. "Is anybody there?" No one answers and every room they try is completely empty. "Perhaps he's not here after all?" suggests Santa. "He might have left the tower and gone off to explore." "Perhaps," agrees Rupert, then he spots a narrow flight of steps leading to the basement. "I wonder?" he murmurs. "If he was down there, he might not be able to hear us call . . ."

At the bottom of the stairs, Rupert and Santa find a cellar with a heavy wooden door . . . "Let me out this instant!" cries an angry voice. "I can't believe I'm being held a prisoner in my own home . . ." "The Professor!" smiles Rupert and reaches for the cellar key. As the door swings open, he sees Bodkin and his old friend, who are both delighted to be set free. "Thank goodness!" sighs the Professor. "For a moment, I thought you were those rascals who locked us up . . ."

RUPERT HEARS WHAT HAPPENED

As Rupert greets the happy pair
They're both amazed that Santa's there . . .

"Our journey into Mirror Land
Just didn't go the way I'd planned . . ."

"Nikdob told my reflection he
Should lock us up immediately!"

"If their machine is like mine, then
It might send us all back again!"

As they leave the cellar, Bodkin and the Professor are astonished to see Santa waiting outside . . . "Hello!" he smiles. "Rupert guessed you might be here, but however did you get into Mirror Land?" "A foolish experiment!" sighs the Professor. "The idea was so fascinating that I never stopped to think what it would be like to meet your own reflection. As soon as the machine was working, Bodkin and I simply stepped through the mirror to find out what lay on the other side . . ."

Explaining how he arrived in Mirror Land, the Professor tells Rupert that he and Bodkin came face to face with their doubles . . . "What a disaster!" he groans. "They weren't at all pleased to see us. Nikdob thought we must be impostors and convinced his master that we'd come to steal his machine!" As soon as he hears that the pair are sound asleep, the Professor is anxious to get back to the laboratory. "If I can reverse the machine, it might take us back to Nutwood!" he declares.

"Oh, dear! They've got the whole thing wrong –
To make it work would take too long . . ."

"Good!" Santa smiles. "Then they'll both stay
On their side while we get away . . ."

"We'll leave them here to slumber on –
They won't wake up until we've gone!"

"Climb in my sleigh. I'll show you how
To get back into Nutwood now . . ."

As soon as they reach the laboratory, the old Professor hurries over to inspect the mirror machine. "Oh dear!" he sighs. "This isn't the same as mine at all! I'm afraid it will never take us back to Nutwood . . ." "Good!" laughs Santa. "Then Nikdob and his master won't be able to follow you there . . ." "But how will we get home?" asks Rupert. "Don't worry," smiles Santa. "There's another way out of Mirror Land. Follow me, everyone!"

At the top of the tower, Rupert and the Professor find Nikdob and his master still slumbering by the fire. "When they wake up the whole thing will seem like a dream!" chuckles Santa. "It serves them right for trying to lock you up!" Leading the way to the roof, he points towards his sleigh. "One more flight and you'll all be back in Nutwood . . ." "Fancy that!" marvels Bodkin. "I once heard sleigh bells on Christmas Eve, but I never dreamt I'd ride in Santa's sleigh . . ."

RUPERT RETURNS TO NUTWOOD

The reindeer all begin to fly
At full speed through the starry sky.

"Look!" Rupert gasps. "They're heading for
A massive archway – like a door!"

Thick fleecy cloud surrounds the sleigh
Then clears as it speeds on its way.

"We're back!" cries Rupert happily.
This time it's Nutwood I can see . . ."

The moment everyone is safely aboard, Santa calls to his reindeer, who soar up into the night sky . . . "Astounding!" gasps the Professor. "I'd no idea that reindeer could fly so fast!" Ahead of them Rupert spots a vast archway, set on a shimmering cloud. "It looks like a giant mirror!" he blinks. "Exactly!" chuckles Santa as the reindeer fly towards it and disappear from sight. "We're leaving Mirror Land behind us now and passing through a gateway to the real Nutwood . . ."

As Santa's sleigh plunges through the archway it is engulfed in a dense, white cloud . . . "Onward!" he cries to the reindeer until they suddenly emerge into brilliant sunshine. "We're back in Nutwood!" cries Rupert. "I can see the whole village spread out below – and everywhere's covered in snow . . ." "Just as you left it!" nods Santa. "All that remains now is to take you back to the Professor's tower." "Hurrah!" cheers Bodkin as they swoop towards it. "We're home at last!"

RUPERT SAYS GOODBYE

"Goodbye!" calls Santa. "I must go!
It's Christmas Eve tonight, you know!"

The Professor tells Rupert how
He'll dismantle the machine now . . .

The pair thank Rupert once again –
"Thank goodness that you found us then!"

As Rupert hurries home he comes
Across a small group of his chums . . .

As soon as he has set down his passengers, Santa takes off once more, to fly to his castle. "Goodbye!" calls Rupert. "And thank you for bringing us home . . ." Inside the tower, everything is exactly as it was before the journey began. "I don't think we'll be needing this again!" says Bodkin, covering up the mirror machine. "Certainly not!" agrees the Professor. "Enough of meddling with reflections! From now on, I intend to leave Mirror Land to Nikdob and his master!"

Now the mystery has been solved, Rupert decides it is time that he was getting home. "I must have been away for ages!" he gasps. "Thank you for all your help!" calls his friend. "If you hadn't come to look for us, Bodkin and I might still be stranded in Mirror Land . . ." Crossing the Common, Rupert spots a group of chums playing in the snow. "This time it's really them!" he laughs delightedly and hurries over to tell his pals all about his strange adventure . . .

RUPERT OPENS HIS PRESENTS

He tells them where he's been, but they
Just won't believe he's been away!

His parents hear his tale and seem
To think the whole thing's been a dream . . .

Next morning, Rupert wakes to find
The presents Santa's left behind.

"My scarf!" he laughs delightedly.
"Now Santa's given it to me!"

"Hello!" calls Rupert as he joins the others. "You'll never guess where I've been!" To his dismay, none of them seem to believe his story. "Really!" laughs Bill. "You're having us on! You can't possibly have done all that – it's not even lunchtime yet . . ." When he gets home, Rupert's parents don't believe in Mirror Land either. "You must have been dreaming!" smiles his father. "Perhaps I was," thinks Rupert as he hangs up his Christmas stocking. "It does seem strange . . ."

Next morning, Rupert wakes to find a stocking full of wonderful presents at the foot of his bed. "Santa's been!" he cries and starts to unwrap them excitedly. Along with all the other gifts, he is intrigued to find a small, flat parcel with something soft inside . . . "My scarf!" he laughs as he tears it open. "The one I gave to Santa! So I did go to Mirror Land after all. It wasn't just a dream . . ."

THE END

114

Rupert's Crossword Puzzle

See if you can complete this crossword. Most of the answers can be found in stories from this year's annual . . .

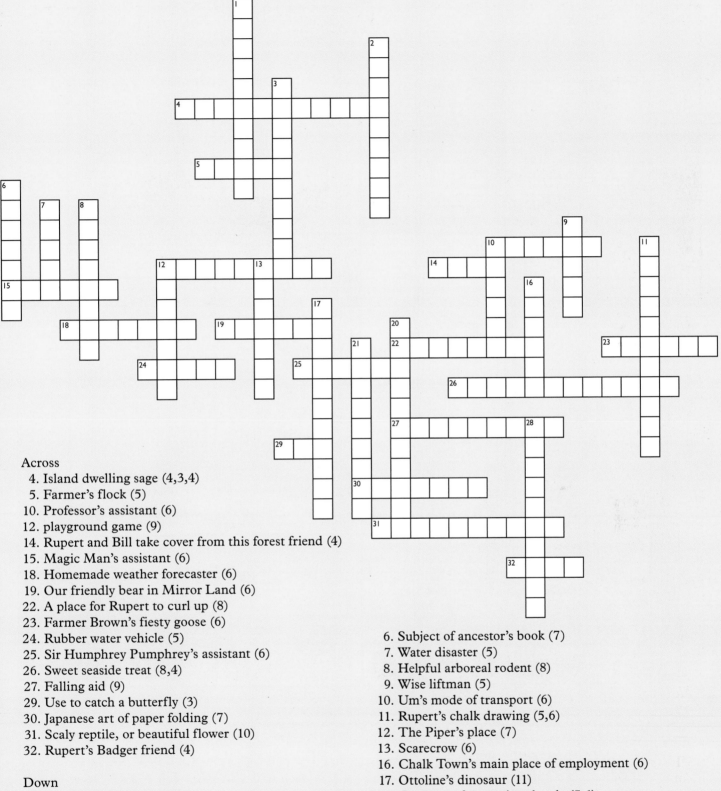

Across

4. Island dwelling sage (4,3,4)
5. Farmer's flock (5)
10. Professor's assistant (6)
12. playground game (9)
14. Rupert and Bill take cover from this forest friend (4)
15. Magic Man's assistant (6)
18. Homemade weather forecaster (6)
19. Our friendly bear in Mirror Land (6)
22. A place for Rupert to curl up (8)
23. Farmer Brown's fiesty goose (6)
24. Rubber water vehicle (5)
25. Sir Humphrey Pumphrey's assistant (6)
26. Sweet seaside treat (8,4)
27. Falling aid (9)
29. Use to catch a butterfly (3)
30. Japanese art of paper folding (7)
31. Scaly reptile, or beautiful flower (10)
32. Rupert's Badger friend (4)

Down

1. Town near Nutwood (10)
2. Colourful winged insect (9)
3. Santa's magic snoozing powder (6,4)
6. Subject of ancestor's book (7)
7. Water disaster (5)
8. Helpful arboreal rodent (8)
9. Wise liftman (5)
10. Um's mode of transport (6)
11. Rupert's chalk drawing (5,6)
12. The Piper's place (7)
13. Scarecrow (6)
16. Chalk Town's main place of employment (6)
17. Ottoline's dinosaur (11)
20. Contents of mysterious bottle (5,6)
21. Legendary outlaw (5,4)
28. Springy jumping surface (10)

Rupert's Memory Game

After you have read all the stories in this book, you can play Rupert's fun Memory Game! Study the pictures below. Each is part of a bigger picture you will have seen in the stories. Can you answer the questions at the bottom of the page? Afterwards, check the stories to discover if you were right.

Now Try to Remember ...

1. What is happening here?
2. Where can this creature be found?
3. What is this?
4. Who drew this chalk creation?
5. Whose hat is the goose wearing?
6. What message did this bird have?
7. What trick is Madera performing?
8. What is Rupert doing?
9. Who are the chums singing for?
10. Where can you find this plant?
11. What has happened here?
12. Where can this object be found?
13. Who gave Rupert this storybook?
14. Where does this bird live?
15. Who threw this and what is it?
16. Who are these presents for?

FOLLOW YOUR LEADER
RUPERT
IN THE
DAILY EXPRESS
EVERY MORNING

Published by the London Express Newspaper Ltd., and
Printed by L.T.A. Robinson Ltd., London, S.W.9
Printed by Greycaines, Watford and London.